EROTIC ROMANCE

MOLLY'S *Daughter*

LILITH JONES

WARNING

This book contains sexually explicit scenes and adult language. It may be considered offensive to some readers. This book is for sale to adults ONLY.

* * * * * * * * * * * * * * * * * * *

Please store your files wisely where they cannot be accessed by underage readers.

Please feel free to send me an email. Just know that these emails are filtered by my publisher. Good news is always welcome.

Lilith Jones - **lilith_jones@awesomeauthors.org**

About the Publisher

4Fun Publishing, a member of **BLVNP Incorporated**, 340 S. Lemon #6200, Walnut CA 91789, info@blvnp.com / legal@blvnp.com

NOTE: Due to the highly emotional reaction of some people to works of erotic fiction, any email sent to the above address that contains foul language or religious references is automatically deleted by our anti-spam software and will not be seen. All other communications are welcome.

DISCLAIMER

Please don't be stupid and kill yourself. This book is a work of FICTION. Do not try any new sexual practice that you find in this book. It is fiction and not to be confused with reality. Neither the author nor the publisher or its associates assume any responsibility for any loss, injury, death or legal consequences resulting from acting on the contents in this book. Every character in this book is over 18 years of age. The author's opinions are not to be construed as the opinions of the publisher. The material in this book is for entertainment purposes ONLY. Enjoy.

Molly's Daughter
Erotic Romance

By: Lilith Jones

© Lilith Jones 2014
ISBN: 978-1-68030-088-8

After the lunch crowd had gone, Anne Bernard watched Mom from the window of the diner until she got to the house. Minutes later, Mom called that she was lying down.

Mom had handled the diner for years by herself. Anne hadn't appreciated how much work it was. Even when she had helped after school, she had bitched at how hard she worked instead of seeing the killing hours Mom had worked. And, then, she'd left Mom to handle it herself for three school years while she was in college. Mom had lied to her about the cancer when she was home for Christmas, though she could tell Mom wasn't feeling healthy.

Now, Mom still came in for lunch and dinner hours. It was Molly's Diner, and Molly still kept it up.

***

Greg Thibault shook the cell phone in his hand. He kept from throwing it across the mesa by telling himself that that would only make the situation worse. And a worse situation than the present would be unbearable. Every arrangement which had been "of course, Professor Thibault," or "no problem, Greg," when he had been in Boulder was unraveling at the other end of an unreliable connection.

"Look," he said, "I'll call you back in an hour or two with better reception." He punched off. He didn't know whether the guy at the department had heard him, but they would know that he wasn't on the line.

The phone companies boasted that they covered 99% of the people living in the country. This mesa was in the 1%. To be fair to the phone companies, not that Greg felt like being fair to any phone companies right then, the Anasazi weren't actually living in the United States. The last of them had been dead five centuries now.

He gave elaborate instructions to his students, descended by the footpath, and headed out in his Jeep. He took a quarter hour to get to something paved. The Jeep was supposed to be an off-the-road vehicle. It's just that the mesa was further off the road than the Jeep had been designed for. He found that his AC was dead, but he would have to climb back up the mesa and down again to get the keys for another vehicle. He opened the windows and got hot, moving air.

He wondered vaguely just why he'd bothered with giving the directions. Being a programming executive described as "like herding cats." Supervising archeological graduate students was like that, but worse. Everybody knew how to do the job better than the instructor did.

The nearest cellphone tower was between the two small towns of Randolph and Copper City. Randolph, the closer one, was more than an hour away. Even so, he passed only three cars on his way. Archeology got done in dry, empty country. It wasn't that Minnesota hadn't had cultures living in the area for millennia; it was that most of their artifacts had rotted or sunk into the ground. When the Anasazi had tossed out a potsherd, it was still where they'd tossed it.

He pulled into the parking lot of a diner in Randolph and called again. His hassles had only begun, and he spent half an hour on the cell, mostly on hold. By then, sweat was running down his body and pooling in the seat of his pants.

Hot, still air was worse than hot, moving air. And the air down here was, if anything, hotter than the air on the mesa. He looked across at Molly's Diner. He had seen the air conditioner when he'd driven in. His glasses were too streaked with his sweat now, but he could hear it when he listened. He'd been an idiot. He would go in and ask to make the other calls from there.

He'd left before lunch. He hadn't missed much. Assigning cooking duties only to coeds would be arrant sexism. On the other hand, guys who were going to major in Anthro didn't take home-ec in high school. Most girls who were going to major in Anthro didn't take home-ec either. Or, if his present students had, they had forgotten everything they'd learned in that course.

The diner had an air conditioner. He could hear it. He'd eat and make the rest of his calls from there. He headed into the diner.

***

Anne didn't recognize the customer who came in. The non-local customers were truckers. How had an 18-wheeler got into the lot without her hearing it? The guy looked rugged, but not like a trucker, and she didn't know why for a minute. Then she did. He was tanned, deeply tanned, but the tone was even. Truckers had more tan on the left side.

She grabbed a menu, and the guy sat at the counter. She got behind the counter and handed him the menu. He took off his glasses and held the menu close.

"The home-made chile looks good," he said. "Might I have some of that?"

"Coffee?"

Greg shivered, and it wasn't the AC. That voice was the sexiest voice he'd ever heard. And she wasn't trying to be sexy. She had only asked if he wanted coffee.

"Please."

Anne poured him his coffee before getting the chile. Truckers, and many locals, were more interested in the coffee than in the food. She'd learned to brew good coffee. That meant pouring out a lot and alternating pots and scrubbing them often. A cup of coffee brought in more than making a pot cost, though, and truckers chose to stop based on the quality of the coffee.

Greg liked the coffee. The chile was the best-tasting food he'd had since he'd come to the mesa. Better than that, it tasted good. He got a napkin out of the dispenser and wiped off his glasses. The waitress was the sexiest woman he'd ever seen. And it was neither her attitude nor her clothes.

She was wearing a blouse that covered her to the elbows and an apron over that. He'd spent the last two weeks with girls wearing shorts and halters, and none of them had been so attractive. The waitress had long hair, but it was tied up in a bun with a pencil stuck in it.

She hadn't presented the bill, but he paid with a $20. She brought him back his change. She stayed within sight while he ate, and that was easy on the eyes.

"Look, ma'am," he said, "the air is out in my Jeep. I have some calls to make from this area. I've been working in a dead zone." He held up his cell. "Would you mind if I made them from that table back there?"

Anne said, "Go right ahead. Want more coffee?"

"Please." This guy had said please more often to her in the last ten minutes than some regular customers had in the last month. She couldn't figure him. He didn't have a local accent. Something in his speech reminded her of the professors at Tempe, though they hadn't been that polite. He looked like he sweated every day in the sun, and he sounded like he spent his life in a library.

He stood at the counter until she had refilled his cup. Then he carried it to a table by the door. By the air conditioner, too, she noticed.

He talked on his cell. He'd been right that he had some calls to make. After the second, he drained his cup and put it down. She carried the pot to his table to refill the cup.

"You didn't have to do that," he said. "I could have gone back for it."

"I wait tables."

"And cook?"

"And sweep the place out at night," she said. "This place barely supports Mom and me. It couldn't pay for a big staff." How barely it supported them, she wasn't going to tell a stranger, however nice he talked.

"Well, I don't know about the sweeping, but if you cooked that chile, you did a damned fine job."

"Why, thank you."

A trucker came in for coffee and pie just then, and she didn't pay attention to the guy until the trucker was served. The guy got loud on the phone towards the end, though, and she could hear that. Apparently, he could tell.

"A lady can overhear me, which puts a real crimp in my vocabulary. But you can take the next down handbasket." The person at the other end apparently said something. "No. Both of you are women, but only one is a lady."

After he closed the cell, he brought his cup to the counter for more coffee and ordered a hamburger. He waited there for the burger, paid, and waited for his change. The driver went out and the guy went back to his table. He made another call and argued some more.

Greg was perfectly well aware that yelling on the phone didn't make them hear you any better. Sometimes, though, he couldn't resist. Finally, he ended his last conversation with Boulder and closed the cell. He brought his cup and saucer back to the counter.

"What sorts of pie do you have?"

Anne said,"Peach, apple, and cherry. We don't cook the pies, though." She couldn't figure why she'd said the last. Just that the guy had said nice things about the chile.

"I'll risk some cherry, anyway. And more coffee." She got the coffee and the pie. He paid immediately, using some of the change she'd given him earlier. She suddenly wondered whether the $20 bill was all the money he'd brought with him.

Greg ate the pie slowly. He told himself that he wanted to stay because of the coolness. The waitress was great to look at, and great to listen to, though she hardly spoke to him. Still, she was a pretty girl in a town full of young men. She was certain to be taken. He could look, but not touch.

"You were right," he said, pushing an empty plate and an empty cup away. "The pie was not home cooked. Nothing wrong with it, though. This is a nice place, how long are you open?"

That, he thought, was real suave, Thibault, not! 'When do you get off?' Indeed. The question isn't when she gets off, but where you get off.

"We're open six to ten."

"Thanks." He put a couple of bills under the edge of his plate and walked towards the door. "Really, thanks for everything," he said before going out. It would be a long drive back, and into the setting sun, too.

Anne said, "You're welcome," in a voice which was probably too low for him to hear. Then she got his dishes, spoon, and fork into the soaking water. There wouldn't be many customers before supper. She might as well wash the dishes now, so she did.

She put the tip into the cash register. About half the truckers and a quarter of the locals tipped. Their tips seldom folded. Of course, the guy had eaten a lot, and he had asked about making calls from here. But people called on cells from the diner all the time. Two free refills weren't a lot, and he sure hadn't made her walk. She did hear his car leave, though she hadn't heard it arrive.

Well, she'd tell Karen about the mysterious stranger in September, and she would invent one of her marvelous stories to explain him. Then Anne stopped smiling. Would she go back to school in September? Would she ever see Karen again? Mom needed her, and when she had needed Mom, Mom had come through. She now realized that she had always needed Mom, despite what she'd thought in high school.

She still needed Mom, and how long would she have her?

Well, this wasn't the last day. Mom came in at 5:30, and they prepared for the rush starting at 6:00. Mom tottered off home at some time after 8:30. Their deal was that Mom would leave when the rush ended, and Anne would close up. After she swept the dust out, she locked up and walked home. Mom always left the porch light on for her evenings, and it lit the entire path.

Then she did the laundry and dropped into bed. At least, with the diner, she never had to cook meals at home.

***

Greg rose when the sun was barely peeking over the horizon. By the time that it had cleared the mesa to the east, the camp was humming. They had a generator, but it wasn't enough to provide illumination for night-time excavation. Days were, of course, longer in the summertime. They weren't as much longer as his upbringing led him to expect. Still, it was a good, long day for excavation and inspection of what they found.

On this site, the interesting finds were less artifacts than the shape of the buildings. Distinguishing mud brick from dirt that had accumulated against it and over it in the succeeding centuries called for judgment and acumen. Even so, they used shovels and even some picks for most of the digging. The proverbial whisk brooms were only used next to the old walls.

When the sun was so far down that the trenches were in shadow, Greg called a halt for supper. This was a far worse meal than he'd eaten in Randolph. Well, he could go there for another bowl of chile. The diner closed at 10:00. He headed down the path at 8:15.

He both walked faster and drove faster than he'd done the day before. He got to the diner before 9:30. The same waitress was there, and there was space at the counter. He ordered another bowl of chile and a cup of coffee. He watched her work until the few remaining customers started toward the door.

"I'm sorry," the waitress said. "It's closing time."

Anne thought that the guy's returning was even more mysterious than his appearing in the first place. He didn't live in Randolph or even close; she would have heard if somebody new had moved in. He sat at the counter until she had to tell him to leave. She cleaned up, swept out the dust, and locked the door.

"Don't be frightened," the guy said from a good way away. She jumped even so. "I just thought I'd offer you a drive home." He moved out so she could see him, though the diner's lights were out. He wasn't moving toward her, and her phone was in her pocket. She got it out and held her finger over the speed dial for 911. She thought it would work up here, too.

"See, that light?" She pointed toward the porch light Mom had left on. "That's a damn short drive."

"Yeah," he said, "my car isn't much closer. May I walk you home, then?"

"Sure." Whatever he could do on a walk home, he could do here and now. Anyway, close enough Mom could hear her scream. She started off, and he caught up with her. "If you're going to walk me home, you can explain yourself."

"Surely, I'm not the only guy who has wanted to walk with you."

"No! Who are you? I might not ever get to describe you to Karen, and I want to know how a guy who looks like a ditch-digger talks like a professor."

"Karen?" he asked.

"My dorm sister. You first. I asked first."

"And so you did. Anyway, you got it in one. An archeologist is a guy who digs ditches with a whisk broom, and I'm a professor of Archeology. Now, you. What's a dorm sister?"

"That's not an explanation," she said. "That's a conundrum. I think I know what an archeologist is, and he isn't a ditch-digger." She stopped to keep from waking Mom with the sound, though every time she lowered her voice, he lowered his.

"Well, since you insist. The Canadians call Indians 'The First Nations.' That's a euphemism like our 'Native Americans.' But really the nations which were here when Columbus ran into the continent on his way to the Indies weren't the first nations here by a long shot. Humans come in cultures like peas come in pods. The guys who crossed the Bering land bridge probably came in organized societies. Hell! Read Jane Goodall. Our cousins the chimps come in organized societies."

Greg suddenly saw that he was talking way too much. There was the loveliest voice on the planet within earshot, and he was drowning it out with Intro to Archeo-America lectures.

"Anyway," he finished, "we dig up remnants -- scraps -- of what those societies used. And, now, what's a dorm sister?"

"Well, if sororities can have sorority sisters, then dormitories can have dormitory sisters."

"Makes sense to me. You're in college, then."

"Yes." Her tone sounded sad. What could be sad about being in college? Infuriating, yes. But sad? "Anyway, I have to go in now. Thanks for walking me home." She walked up to the porch and into that light. Her hips looked especially enticing as she walked through the door.

Anne thought that she was home safe, but Mom spoke out of the darkness.

"What was that?"

"Guy at the diner walked me home."

"Who was he?"

"I don't know," she said. Not explaining how much she didn't know. "Some professor."

"At the diner?"

"That was what I wanted to know, but he started explaining in 1492 and went backward."

"He was evading your questions?" Mom asked. "I don't want you talking to him." Mom always thought guys were trying to seduce her. A little projection there. Sure the high school boys had been out for what they could get, but they hadn't aimed specifically at her. If you wore a skirt, a high school boy wanted to lift it.

"He wasn't evading my questions, Mom. He was a professor. I've spoken with professors before. They're harmless." This professor hadn't looked harmless, though. He'd looked tough and sexy as hell, and tall. Still, he hadn't even touched her, and she would never see him again.

She did see him the next night, though. He ordered more chile and another cup of coffee. Seeing as refills were free, he getting only one cup wasn't as complimentary to the coffee as he was to the chile.

"Closing time," she said to him when 10:00 rolled around.

"Well, can I do something to help you close up? Dry dishes?" If he was planning to walk her home, she would be more happy with him on the inside than waiting in the dark.

"Well, you're an expert with brooms. You can sweep up." She handed him the broom and dustpan and he went to work.

"It's a very short drive," he said when she was finished. "Still, if I drive you home, we can sit in the car while we talk." He was persistent, but that was okay. She wanted to hear more from him. Lectures were more interesting when you weren't going to be tested on them.

"So," she said when they were sitting in his Jeep, "what got you marooned out here?"

"Well, I said I study ancient American cultures. One of the ones which left significant remnants is the Anasazi. They had a settlement on top of Long Mesa. That's some miles west of here. I'm directing an excavation of that settlement. This is the closest still-existent town."

"And you decided to come into town every night?"

"Now, you know better than that. I came to town because I know you get cell service. The mesa doesn't. Since then, I came back to see you."

"And not to eat chile?" she asked. She needed some breathing room after the last statement.

"Well, the chile is part of the experience. But I wouldn't drive an hour for that chile, as excellent as it is. Anyway, you know all about me. What about you?"

Anne didn't think she knew anything about him. She knew he was a professor of archeology, that he drove a Jeep, and that he talked smoothly. That was hardly a biography.

"I don't know anything about you. What is your name?"

Greg said, "Greg Thibault." He pronounced it Tea-Bow. "And what's yours?"

"Anne Bernard."

"I've told you my field. It's Archeology. What's your major."

"History," she said. "I was going to teach history in high school."

Greg heard that "I was." He could tell that there was an something important hidden in those words. He didn't consider himself a sensitive man, but he could also tell that he shouldn't ask.

"So," he said, "tell me some significant historical fact."

"When the confederates invaded the territory of New Mexico, they called their short-lived conquest 'Arizona.'"

"Okay. Now tell me some significant fact about Anne Bernard."

"She is due to open a diner," she said, "with the coffee made and the oatmeal cooking, in less than eight hours."

Anne didn't know why she'd said that. She was enjoying the conversation, even after he'd asked her major.

"Okay." He started the Jeep and drove the few yards to her house. "Stay there. I'll help you out." He did, and walked her to the porch door. Neither said anything as they walked. She had the weirdest temptation to turn for his kiss as she had for other kisses at that door.

Greg wished that she had kissed him good night. He desperately wanted to taste those lips. Still, he hadn't had a date with her.

The next night, he asked for a menu. There was home-made vegetable soup on offer, and he took that. He swept out the place and walked her to the Jeep.

"So," he asked, "what do the kids around here do to amuse themselves?" He didn't want to ask her for a date and then ask her where to go. He figured "kids" was safe enough. He realized he wasn't being as subtle as he was trying to be. Damn it! Subtlety wasn't his long suit.

Anne realized he wasn't trying to be suggestive. The fact was that the county had one of the highest illegitimate-birth rates in the state, and that didn't even count shotgun weddings. The Sociology professor in Tempe had said it was because the kids in high school didn't have any other amusements.

"Well," she said, "there used to be a movie theater in Copper City, but it closed. The high school holds dances during the school year. Mostly, though, people watch TV. Sometimes, they watch it together."

"Well, this is a Jeep, not a Delorian." What did that mean? "Is the diner open seven days a week?" She saw that he wanted to ask her out. He had, really, asked her out. It was just that they had no place to go but to sit in this Jeep.

"We open at noon on Sundays."

"So you can go to church?" he asked.

That was a sore point. The town was divided between two churches. The Bernards didn't attend either of them.

"We open precisely at noon," she said. "We have to start the coffee and cook the food first." Actually, plenty of people came to eat right after church.

"Still, it's better than six." That was beyond argument. He was silent for a moment. Then, "What's the best thing about teaching high school history?"

"That's hard to say," she began. She saw so many great things, and they all looked so much better as they receded into impossibility. Well, she wouldn't starve. She had, after all, more experience as a waitress and a short-order cook than almost any girl her age. Anyway, he was waiting. "There's a connection. Or is it connectedness? I have so few personal connections, but history connects you to everybody else in the whole world. And it's great to deal with young minds. Oh, sure, some of the kids in high school don't care about any of their subjects."

"Some of the kids in college, too. Go ahead. I was interrupting."

"But, I had teachers who lit a spark. And that's the greatest thing in the world. Karen talks about turning white paper into a story, but when you can turn a human being into an inquisitive student, you've done much more."

"So what," he asked, "is the downside?"

"I can't think of any." He was silent, and she felt she should go on. "I honestly can't."

"Well, I can think of downsides to college teaching, but that's from experience. Still, I do it. Why in hell did you say that you once were going into high school teaching?"

Greg saw that this was a stupid question before it was out of his mouth. He cared for this girl a lot, but that didn't give him the right to interrogate her. He wanted to talk to her, and this question was going to make her hate talking to him. She didn't have to. Probably the woods -- well the town, the closest woods were a hundred miles away -- were full of old boyfriends who would be glad to do her the favor of sending him on his way, with a few bruises if not a load of buckshot. Greg Thibault talked well, and he thought clearly. It's just that he did the first before he did the second.

She burst into tears. He put his arms around her, and -- since she didn't slap his face or punch him in the nuts -- he cradled her while she cried it out.

Anne didn't care that he was a stranger. She couldn't hold it in any longer, and Karen was at the other end of the state. She broke down and laid it out to him as it kept pushing her.

"Mom paid my tuition," she said. "She did everything for me. Now, she can't anymore. Cancer." She had said it. She had said it, and she hadn't been struck by lightning. Greg hadn't even rejected her. It had been two weeks since Mom had told her, and she hadn't said the word in those weeks.

"That sucks."

"And I have to take care of her, now. Her and the diner. It barely supported us before, and there are more expenses, and I can't make it go, and Mom is getting too weak to do what she does, and I'm not strong enough to do it all."

"So, you're not going back in September." He wasn't asking, he was stating.

"And once I stop, I don't know if I can go back."

"Look," he said, "I'm faculty, not administration. Still, I know that schools look at the needs. Dropping out to care for a sick mother is understandable in the way that dropping out to find yourself isn't. They accommodate the second all the time. This is a tragedy, a personal tragedy. Still, it doesn't have to be the end of your education."

"You don't know. Mom borrowed on everything, and I took out student loans. I can't start again in September, and that means that repayments on the student loans became due starting in June. I'll go bankrupt, and that won't apply to student loans."

Greg could tell she was screwed. There had to be some way out, but he didn't see it. So he just held her and patted her back the way he'd held Diane after the accident.

"The diner is our only source of income," she said still in his arms. "And nobody would buy it for what she borrowed against it. The house, too. We have to pay for both to have somewhere to live and something to eat. She's getting weaker, and I can't both care for her and run the diner."

Anne finally straightened up. "You must think me so weak," she said.

"The whole fucking world falls on you, and you carry it. You cry about that happening. That's weakness? I wish I were that strong." He started the Jeep, and drove her home.

She didn't see him Friday night, and was strangely sad. She had depended on him, and then her weeping fit had driven him away.

***

Greg felt sad for Anne. He also felt guilty. That wasn't because he'd made her cry. He thought she had probably needed that cry. But while she had cried, he'd held her in his arms. If she had known what he was thinking then, she would have killed him. She certainly would have felt deeply betrayed. He had taken in his arms -- mostly -- out of sympathy. But, once she was there, his hormones had kicked in viciously.

Still, considering the past after a good night's sleep, he thought that he wasn't too bad an influence on her. She had needed that period of crying; she had needed that cuddling while she was crying. His motivation was beside the point. Then, too, his motivation going in had been relatively pure. His sensations when he did it were what were totally impure.

He would give it a rest for one night, though. Her tears were only the beginnings of her emotional need. She needed to work through her feelings rationally, and he would allow her time for that. Besides, he had plans for Saturday night. He shaved in lukewarm water and packed a blanket down to his Jeep before he headed on Saturday.

***

Anne was surprised when she saw him again Saturday night. He asked for a menu just as though she hadn't spilled her guts two nights back.

"Is the western omelet too much trouble at this time of night?" he asked.

"I cook it to order. It's no harder at night than in the morning." For that matter, business was trailing off by this time. It was easier than in the morning rush.

He stayed and swept out the place again. "Sorry to not do this yesterday," he said. "I figured that I'd been interfering with your rest."

"That's okay." Sweeping out wasn't anything. Not seeing him had interfered more with her rest than their conversations had.

"Well," he said when they got to the Jeep, "you have a chance to sleep in tomorrow. There doesn't seem to be much to do in town, but enjoy nature. Want to go out a bit and look at the stars?"

Mom would be asleep, and she wouldn't know anything. "Okay." He headed out of town a couple of miles. He cut off the road and headed north maybe another quarter of a mile before stopping.

She started to worry when he got a blanket out of the Jeep. Well, he had always taken no for an answer, and if he wouldn't, it was already a long walk back to town. It was better to wait for him to try something than to start off now. He spread out the blanket and turned off the engine and all the lights. He lay down on the blanket on his back.

"Come lie down," he said. "If you look straight up into the sky, you can see millions of stars away from the light pollution of the towns." She lay down a couple inches away, and -- to her surprise -- he kept that distance from her.

"You know," he said after the stars had begun to multiply, "I lost my parents when I wasn't much older than you are now. It wasn't the same, there wasn't the agony of seeing it coming. The whole family was gathered for Christmas; Dad and Mom went out for some last-minute shopping; they were dead on arrival before we ever heard that there had been an accident. At the time, that didn't seem merciful. Compared to your situation, it was."

"You have a large family?"

"You might say so. There are four of us kids. I was the eldest, and that was a conflict. Dad wanted me to go into the family business. When I wouldn't, Norman took part in it. He majored in economics, and had entered Wharton for an MBA. After Dad and Mom died, he took the reins of the company with hardly any apprenticeship."

"Are you very close?" she asked. That sounded like an ideal existence to her. Greg had enjoyed two parents. He hadn't lost either until he was out of college. He'd had a close bunch of brothers and sisters to celebrate Christmas with. The family business sounded like it was still operating, and he didn't have to do anything to make it go.

"Not really. I'm in Colorado. I mean I'm here, but I usually teach in Colorado. Norman is back in Minnesota. Diane is finishing up med school in Maryland. Ross, the afterthought, is still an undergraduate in Illinois. We get together sometimes, but it's mostly to argue. Anyone else but your mother and you?"

"No. I don't remember my father." She had come to doubt Mom's story and her wedding ring. Still, however much she trusted Greg, you don't tell anyone that your Mom's public story is a lie. Anyway, what she had said was the truth. She had had a father, and she didn't remember him. What she omitted was guesswork, and it wasn't her story. "It was always the two of us. Mom's been operating the diner as long as I can remember. That's named after her, Molly."

"A hard life," he said.

"Yeah. And I didn't realize how hard. She did the cooking and handled most of it while I bitched about waiting tables for the evening hours. And that was high school. When I was younger, she handled all of it and handled raising me. Maybe I ate in the diner, but she shopped for clothes and washed clothes and tended me while I was sick."

"She loved you," he said. He sounded like he believed that what Mom had done was what you did for someone you love.

"Anyway," he continued, "you have to see that my family has another sort of relationship. I certainly didn't expect Dad to die, and neither, for that matter, did Norman. He expected the old man to stay on as chairman of the board after he hit 65, but make Norman the president. Instead, he's both. He keeps claiming that I was disloyal for not going into the company, but he would have been miserable if I had. I would be the president, now, and he'd be something like vice president for marketing. And we'd disagree about business decisions -- we disagree about everything else -- and I'd be in charge.

"That's my side. He doesn't see it that way."

"And your sister?"

"Well, they never planned on putting her in the company. She used to try to help hurt animals and birds. Even some insects. The big surprise is that she's now interested in treating humans.

"And my brother Ross was an afterthought. Mom and Dad never admitted to us that he was a failure in contraception, although I've suspected that. You're eleven, and suddenly your mother is pregnant. He was either being babied or being bullied. Even Diane spanked him at times when he was in the early grades. Then, too, he was an orphan much younger than the rest of us. Norman took control, took responsibility, Norman would say. Nowadays, he is in engineering and doesn't want to take sides.

Greg continued. "I'll tell you how divisive my family is. I told you my name is pronounced tea-bow. Well, that's the original French pronunciation." He told her how to spell it. "The company has been called 'Thigh-Balt Milling' for decades. Norman keeps that pronunciation of his name. Diane and I have gone back to the French. Ross answers to either. He doesn't want to take sides."

Anne said, "Families are of all different sorts." She could remember seeing other families and envying the kids for having two parents. Then some of those families had split.

"So," he asked, "what is a dormitory sister like?"

"Well, her dormitory sister is like me, and you know me." She was so pedestrian. "But Karen is a dream as a roommate. We will walk past somebody, maybe a couple kissing goodbye, maybe a man raising a ruckus about some purchase he made in a store. When we get back to the dorm, she'll tell me an elaborate story about them. The woman in the kissing couple is in the reserves and has just been called for active duty. They are storing a fertilized egg in a bath of liquid nitrogen at home in case she doesn't come back. The man is a secret agent who lost his micro-copy of the secret he'd stolen in something he'd purchased and returned. He wants that particular object back."

Greg asked, "She's some kind of a psychic? How does she know all this?" And why, he wondered, did that sort of drama happen in Tempe of all places? He'd bet the total population of spies in Tempe could be counted on one hand.

"Oh, she makes them up. But every detail that you notice she can explain in her scenario. I was going to ask her about you. How come a guy who looked like he worked in the sun all day sounded like he lived in a library?"

"Is there any reason you can't ask her anyway?" he asked. "I'll give you my email, and you can send me the explanation. I'd be fascinated to hear what I sound like to her -- a lot more romantic than the real pedestrian job I have, I'll wager."

And, of course, if she did send the explanation, he would have her e-mail. He was starting to think subtly. Besides, the longer Anne talked about Karen the longer she was thinking about something else besides her own problems.

Anne thought that it was endearing that Greg considered his job pedestrian. He was, after all, a real-life Indiana Jones. Maybe he didn't have the whip or face the conspirators, but he was a real archeologist. She rolled over and kissed him for that.

Greg was astonished by the kiss. The surprise didn't freeze him, though. He grabbed Anne and pulled her into a serious kiss. He hugged her on top of his body while he licked her lips then kissed their corners.

Anne hadn't actually intended the kiss to go this far, but she was thrilled when it did. She greeted his tongue with her own and held his head to pull him into the kiss. Her mind didn't even acknowledge her body's being pressed against his, but her body responded by spreading her legs. She felt her nipples hardening.

When his hands went to her breasts, though, a learned response kicked in. She pushed that arm with both of hers. She had wrestled amorous boys before, and she wondered if she would have to kick hard to make this amorous boy let go.

Instead, he dropped his hands. The one she was pressing against went loose so fast that she dropped with her shoulder against his chest.

"I'm sorry," he said. "I don't know what came over me."

"You don't have to apologize." He had, after all, stopped immediately. And she had started the kiss. She rolled over on her back again. "I thought that we came to look at the stars."

"Yeah." And he began to point out constellations.

Greg couldn't believe that she had forgiven him for that clumsy near-rape. He looked at his cell after a bit and saw that more than an hour had passed since closing time. She had more time on Saturday nights, but not infinite time.

"I probably should get you back," he said. He shook out the blanket while she got in the Jeep. When he'd walked her to the door, she turned to face him. He was not only going to be forgiven, he was going to be allowed a good-night kiss. He cupped her face in both hands and kissed her gently. Keeping his hands off the rest of her would be easier if they had some place they should be.

Anne had established that he would obey limits. She wasn't sure that she could. The kiss was hotter than the earlier one, and she nearly melted. When she was able to move back, though, he let her go. She got in the door, stripped, and dropped into bed. She had dreams that night, but she enjoyed each of them.

Sunday, Greg spent leading the team in sorting out what the dig had learned in the past week and what they would do in the next week to do more. The crew wasn't a religious bunch, but they appreciated having one day a week when they didn't have to dig.

That night, he was in the diner. She not only accepted him, she gave him more tasks. Before sweeping out, he filled the napkin dispensers and the salt and pepper shakers.

"Look," he said afterwards in the Jeep, "I don't think I've been giving you enough sleeping time. Why don't we say I'll be here Tuesday, Thursday, Saturday, and Sunday?" She nodded without actually saying anything. "And Saturday, we'll look at the stars again?"

"Oh, yes. I saw lots of stars last night." Anne was clearly an innocent, but he couldn't interpret that sentence as anything other than a double entendre. For that matter, it was more a one-and-a-half entendre. The innocent meaning was quite a stretch.

That night, too, she gave him a good-night kiss. He explored her mouth quite thoroughly before she pulled away. He was happy going home, much less happy the next night staying in. He, too, though, needed his sleep.

Tuesday night, he went into town before heading home. He didn't really think that this romance was going to go all that far, especially so soon. If it did, however, he would be a monster if he wasn't prepared. He couldn't believe a woman like Anne was on the pill. It was his responsibility to take precautions.

When he had been a carefree graduate student, he had never gone on a dig without two packs of condoms. Three, when he was going to Mexico with no knowledge of how to get them locally. There were years he'd brought them back unopened. There were also years when he'd had to replenish his supply.

He was a responsible director of the dig this year, though. Playing around with one of his students would violate all sorts of rules as well as professional ethics. So, he had come without. What he hadn't anticipated was a local, and such a beautiful local, too. Well, she had said no, once, but she was giving him good-night kisses every night now.

Anyway, the town had a drug store, closed as late as he'd dropped Anne off. When he stopped there on his way Thursday, it was already closed, but he looked at the shopping times on the sign on the front door. It would close on Saturday at 9:00, which was earlier than he usually got to the diner. On Saturday, he got in the drug store at 8:45.

"Trojans, please," he said to the druggist. "A box of twelve if you have them." The druggist had them, and Greg paid. In his Jeep, he got out one packet and put it in a shirt pocket where it wouldn't fall out at an inappropriate time. He put the rest of the box in the glove compartment.

He got to the diner early, and had two cups of coffee and a bowl of chile. He swept out the dust and walked her to the Jeep. When they lay on the blanket in the dark, they looked up at the stars and watched the faintest slowly appear as their eyes adjusted. He reached over and held her hand.

Anne felt comforted. She had come on this date expecting to spend the time kissing, and maybe they would. But Greg wasn't pushing her. Greg felt that her hand was worth holding and not just the sexier parts. She pulled his hand to her mouth and kissed it. He pulled her hand across to his mouth and kissed her fingers.

"I keep thinking," she said, "that you're the right man for me. But this is definitely the wrong time."

"I'm not sure," he said. "You have to take care of her. Who is going to take care of you while you do? I may not be much help with the physical stuff. Sweeping the floor and filling the pepper shakers isn't one percent of what you do. But I can listen. Who else do you have to talk to?"

"Not Mom. She used to say that I could talk to her about anything. Well, I never talked to her about some things, but even they would have been easier than talking to her about her illness."

Greg was happy to hear that she hadn't talked about some things. Clearly, it was what she'd done with boys. Sometimes Anne acted or sounded so innocent. Well, if she'd done things with boys she hadn't told her mother, then she wasn't all that innocent. He didn't have to worry about how far he could go with her. How far she would go with him was another question. She had proved herself capable of saying no, all he had to do was respect that. Since he didn't have to worry about controlling himself otherwise, he relaxed.

Anne felt that relaxation, and it calmed her. She had appreciated his kisses this past week, and she had thought that kissing was what they had come here for. She didn't want to talk about Mom, now. She did want to talk about them, but what could you say about them? They didn't have a past worth discussing -- a couple of weeks. They didn't have a future. She had to care for Mom as long as she lived. Talking about after she was dead was too painful, to say nothing of the macabre.

If she could talk to Greg about Mom, she certainly couldn't talk to Mom about Greg. She had always been overprotective about boys. Most of her friends had protective moms with too-strict rules. Mom, though, had gone to extremes. When Anne had gone with boys and parked on the way home, Mom hadn't treated it as defiance, like all the other breaking of rules that Anne did. She had treated it like a threat to them both. And the way the boys treated her like a prize to be won instead of a person to be cherished had scared her as much as Mom had.

But, if she couldn't talk to Mom about boys, still less could she talk to Greg about them. She missed Karen. She squeezed Greg's hand, though, and rolled over facing him.

Greg felt her movements. When he matched them, they were very close. He kissed her nose tip. When she didn't push him away, he kissed her for real. He had an erection, and he worried about how she would react. When she didn't, he stopped worrying. She tasted sweet, and she felt wonderful. Her back was firm and young and strong under his hand. Her breasts were soft against his chest. Her rump was beautifully rounded. When he gripped it, she flexed it into his hand and pressed her groin into his.

Anne was swept up in the kiss. He tasted a little bit of the chile, but the touch of his tongue on hers was electric. He stroked her back as though she was desirable. She had learned that many boys liked her breasts and her butt. She wasn't sure that they liked her. Greg liked her, and Anne liked him. When his hand did come around to her breast, it was even more exciting.

Then Greg rolled her back. He kissed all over her face, the cheeks, the corner of her eye, her forehead, her ear. That was particularly sensitive, and when he continued down her neck, she shivered. She looked straight up, but some of the stars she saw weren't really up there. As his kisses continued lower, he unbuttoned her blouse to give his lips room. He kissed her, or rather her bra, right between her breasts.

Kisses on her stomach were sexy and ticklish. Kisses on her side were even more of both. When he took her blouse off, he kissed up her right arm from her wrist to her neck. Those were incredibly arousing. So were kisses on the palms of her hands.

"Roll away from me," he said when he was lying beside her again, "so I can get the catches on your bra." When she had and had rolled back, his kisses on her breasts were the most arousing of all. Later, when he had removed her skirt, he stroked the insides of her thighs, stroked them maddeningly slowly -- slowly stroked them until it drove her mad. He stopped to grip the elastic of her panties with both hands.

"Lift up again," he said, "so I can get these off."

"I don't know," she said, and she didn't know how far she wanted to go. He hadn't said that he loved her, and guys did before you bared your breasts. She hadn't necessarily believed them, but she'd expected them to say that. She had never let a guy take her panties off, not in high school and not in three years of college. She had never felt like this with those guys, though, even when they had told her that they loved her -- even when she had told them the same.

"Well," he said, "you have to decide." He was sitting up above her. His hands were still on her panties, but he had stopped kissing her.

"What?"

"You have to decide. I want more. You are an incredibly desirable woman, and I'd like to kiss all of you. That means that how far we go is your decision. But I can't act on 'I don't know.' Do your panties go down or stay up?"

"They stay up," she said. Wasn't he supposed to be wrestling her right now? "Sorry, you don't get what you want."

"Well, since you're setting limits. Your panties stay on. I presume my trousers stay on, too. Can I take my shirt off? I want to feel you with more than my hands. And would you take down your hair?"

"My hair?" She started to take out the bobby pins.

"You have lovely hair. I want to run my hands through it, but I don't want to pull it and have it hurt you." He took off his shirt, though she hadn't really answered that.

Then he was lying on top of her and kissing her again. He leaned to one side and ran his other hand through her hair. He'd been right. This was an even better kiss when his skin was against hers.

He went lower on the blanket and kissed her thighs. First the tops and then the insides. Later, he was beside her, kissing her breasts and stroking between her thighs. When she parted her legs, he scratched with his fingernails across the bottoms of her panties.

The arousal was incredible. He kept scratching and sucked one nipple. She felt her bottom leave the blanket as she arched into that feeling. His finger went beneath her panties and stroked her folds there. When he found her clit, he moved his kisses to her mouth.

She writhed and screamed into his mouth as her orgasm hit. It seemed to last forever.

"Anne, darling. Sweet Anne. Oh, darling," he said. He kissed her forehead and then the tip of her nose. He ran his hand through her hair. He was lying on that side, but she could feel the hand move through her hair a little. "When you're ready," he said.

"I thought you said we weren't going to." Though feeling like this, she didn't think she was up to wrestling with him.

"No, this." He rolled onto his back. He lifted her and placed her on him, still lying on her back. "Am I a little softer than the ground?" He was a little softer, and a lot warmer. She felt his hardness under her butt. His hands were stroking her and then cupping her breasts. This was marvelous, but she worried about the time.

"What time is it?" she asked. He lifted her down and rolled away from her. He pulled his cell phone out of his pocket.

"Twelve fifteen," he said.

Greg was sorry to tell her, because he knew that this ended the evening. She had looked ethereal lying there in the starlight. She even looked ethereal scrambling into her clothes after he had ruined his night vision staring at the time on his cell. He got up, got his shirt back on, and shook out the blanket. The Jeep started easily, and he drove her home.

"Take care," he said after he'd kissed her good night.

Anne felt that she had taken too little care. She certainly got too little sleep. What she had, though, was pleasant and marked with happy dreams.

She got through the day, even though it was a drag. Mom went back to the house at 8:00 and Greg showed up at 9:30. He swept out the diner while she did the dishes. Then he filled the salt and pepper shakers and the napkin dispensers while she took down her hair. She sat on his lap and kissed while he ran his hands through her hair.

"Walk me back," she said. He walked her to the porch and they had one more kiss while he ran his hands through her hair again. He watched her through the door and went back toward his Jeep. She watched him out of sight and went to her room.

"Anne, come in here," Mom said from her room. She should have been asleep, but she didn't even sound tired. The bedside lamp was on.

"It's nearly eleven," Mom said. "You've been gone a long time."

"I had to clean up the diner. You know Sunday is the day for stuff you don't do every day."

"I never took more than a half hour on Sunday evenings."

"So," Anne said, "I don't claim to be as good as you are."

"And I usually did it all by myself. Your hair is down. Where did you do it?"

"I took it down while I was in the diner."

"That's not what I asked," Mom said. "Does he have a camper you do it in? Does he bring something to the diner so you do it on the floor?"

"Mom!" Mom obviously thought they had been having sex.

"Your father didn't die. We were never married. After he learned I was pregnant with you, I never saw him again."

"I sort of knew that." Anne had figured out almost all of that. The detail about not seeing him again after he learned about the pregnancy was new, but not a shock.

"When did you know?"

"It was never one point," Anne said. "I had a friend, Emily. You might remember her. Her dad died in the army. They had nearly a shrine for him in their home. I wondered why you had only the one picture. Is that really him?"

"Yeah," Mom said. She seemed to be waiting for more. Well, better this than talking about Greg.

"When Grandma died and left you that money, she was named Bernard. Then, too, you told me that you'd been estranged; you never said why. And you had a story about how you and Dad met. You never had a story about when you got married. Other moms had pictures of their weddings somewhere. It wasn't one thing, and kids sometimes said it about you."

"They knew? It was a long way from here."

"I don't think they knew. I don't think your generation knew -- knows. I think people guess. I didn't know; I guessed."

"Well," Mom said, "I don't want it to happen to you."

"I don't want it to happen to me, either. It won't."

"Your guy. What is his name?"

"Greg," Anne said. She had told Mom that.

"He bought some rubbers. At the drug store. Yesterday." He did? Why did he do that? Did he want to put up a billboard? Probably, if he had put an ad in the Copper City paper, fewer people in town would know.

"Well, he didn't use them," she said. "Not yesterday. Not today. Today, he barely got his hands below my neck. He mostly ran them through my hair. I won't deny that we made out yesterday -- well, last night. We didn't make love. I've never made love with anybody.

"And I'll tell you this, Mom," she continued. Greg had been so concerned about Mom, and now Mom was so spiteful about Greg. "The reason that I've never had sex -- I won't say it would have been making love -- is that I'm willing to kick and scream to get the boy to stop. Real kicking. It would have been real screaming if I'd thought that would have helped. And I've never had to do that with Greg.

"One time," she continued. There was so much she couldn't talk to Mom about, and she had brought this up. "One time, he asked me to lift up so he could pull down my panties. I said that I didn't know. He said that I would have to say yes or no. So, he accepts a no. He even asks for my decision. So, I'm in control." And there was so little she was in control of.

"I don't want you to wind up like I did."

"Seems to me that makes three of us." After all, idiotic as it was for Greg to buy a contraceptive in town, he had bought a contraceptive. If he didn't want to marry her, he didn't want to leave her to raise a kid all on her own, either.

"You can't trust them when they say that they love you." That was old news, Mom. And Greg wasn't one of the guys who had told her that.

"Seems to me," she said, "that the question is whether you love them."

"Well, you're wrong. The question is whether you're married. If you don't have the ring on your finger, you are on your own when things go wrong." Mom was silent for a bit, and she thought it was time she got a little sleep. She was running a sleep deficit so deep that she might fall asleep while frying eggs tomorrow.

"Oh, Honey," Mom continued, "I didn't mean that you were something which went wrong."

"I didn't think you did. One of us has to have some sleep or the diner won't open tomorrow." When she got to bed, however, she tossed and turned thinking how Greg had betrayed her. Angry as she was at Mom for interfering, Mom needed all her energy to keep herself alive. Greg had wasted a month's worth of Mom's energy by his purchase. And he'd been taking her for granted, too.

Mom said that you had to be married. Karen said that it was okay if you were in love. (Karen had been in love four times in the past three years.) What did Anne say? And was it okay if you were in love and he wasn't? Wasn't that what had really happened to Mom?

She didn't have any answers, and the more she thought the more questions she had.

***

Greg had been very happy about Sunday night. They couldn't have sex, or even make out seriously, when Anne needed to be up at 6:00 the next morning. There only chances were Saturday nights. That was unfortunate, but if it limited his libido, it left his ego untarnished.

He enjoyed talking to her and loved kissing her, too. He had his preferences on which, but Anne had deeper needs just now, and she should have her choice. When she chose kissing, that was a great ego boost. Her hair was gorgeous, and she not only let him play with it, she seemed to enjoy that, too. It was a lovely auburn in the diner lights. It had looked black in the starlight.

He'd said that he would keep away Monday nights, and the last thing he wanted was to drive her to exhaustion. She was so alive that she should keep that vivacity, and exhaustion wasn't the way. Besides, being bad for her was a way to have her decide that he should go.

Tuesday night, when he got to the diner, Anne was barely civil to him. He ate his stew in silence, figuring that she was trying to hide her feelings from the other customers.

"I'm sorry, sir," she said to him icily when 10:00 rolled around, "this is closing time. You have to leave." Well, something had happened, and he would find out what. He waited around the corner of the diner until she had locked the door.

"So," he said in a loud voice, "what happened?" She sped up, but he was between her and the house. He was actually walking a little ahead of her. "Look, you were happy Saturday night. You were happy the next night. Something happened, and I don't know how it could be me. Why are you mad at me because of something somebody else did."

"It was what you did," Anne said. "Can't you keep your voice down? I don't want to wake Mom."

"Sure," he said in a lower voice. "Let's stop here and talk in a conversational tone. So what was it that I did?"

"You bought contraceptives! You thought I was that kind of girl!" She had stopped, but he didn't consider the tone of voice conversational. 'Vituperative' was more like it. She also sounded on the verge of tears. So he had bought condoms, and she knew about the purchase. Well, he hadn't told her. The pharmacist had. Probably indirectly. Almost certainly indirectly. "You know that city dude who's dating Anne? He brought some protection in my store."

"Well, I bought contraceptives in town. That was clearly a stupid move, and I apologize for my stupidity. I'm a city guy, and I think of a purchase as a private matter."

"And you think I'm a slut," she said.

"I don't think that you're a slut. I thought that you were a free woman capable of making a free choice. You made that choice, made a choice, Saturday night. I respected that choice.

"Now," he continued, "I might have preferred that you make another choice. But I had told you that at the time. I wanted you, I wanted you in all ways. Still do, for that matter. You didn't want me as much, and I let you decide, and I respected that decision."

Anne felt that he was twisting everything totally around. She started walking again. He walked along with her, but didn't try to touch her.

"See you Sunday," he said. Sunday? He wasn't giving up, but he wasn't coming to deliver more arguments, either.

She really wouldn't be convinced whatever he said. He'd demeaned her, and she would never give him the time of day, again. On the other hand, she would have preferred him to at least try. He'd said that he wanted her, didn't he want her enough to make an effort?

Greg figured that Anne needed a pause. Thursday was the next scheduled day, and he wouldn't come then. Coming on Saturday implied too much. Saturday had been their day for stargazing and making out. That left Sunday as the next day he could reasonably meet her. Then, too, without him she would presumably get some sleep Saturday night. With a little more sleep, she might look more favorably on him. It also implied that he wasn't only interested in their Saturday-night sessions of making out. He was interested in her.

He actually came to town the next day, but carefully avoided the diner. He drove the Jeep in to the local garage. Gary followed and drove him back while he left the Jeep to get the air fixed.

Anne started feeling that Greg was cheating in not coming at night and arguing with her. That left nobody to argue with but herself. Greg had taken no for an answer, and she had originally thought that was a point in his favor. Still, he'd thought she would go all the way; he'd thought that she was a slut.

Then she thought about Karen. Karen had had sex with four men, and none of them were of Greg's quality. Anne had only known three of them, but Karen's description of her summertime fling hadn't sounded anywhere as fine as Greg was. Greg was a professor, and he had muscles. If Karen had met Greg, she would have fallen for him. And, if she had fallen for him, she would have had sex with him. And Karen was anything but a slut.

Even if Karen hadn't fallen for him, even if Anne had asked Karen's advice as to how she should behave, Karen would have told her to go for it. Then, saying that Anne might have sex with him was saying that Anne was like Karen. It wasn't like Karen in her best ways, but it was like Karen. And, honestly, how was he supposed to know? You don't go around wearing signs: this one can be persuaded; this one can't be persuaded. She'd kicked some shins bloody telling them that she couldn't be persuaded.

That had always been a point in Greg's favor. He could take no for an answer. And he would talk with her. Of course, he would only talk with her because he had thought she could be talked into having sex with him.

But that was attributing more evil to him than he deserved. Even when other guys had figured out that the line she drew was a serious boundary, reaching that line had been the end of the date. When she had established the boundary with Greg, he had wanted more cuddling with her. He hadn't crossed that boundary.

Well, he had pushed the limit. He hadn't taken down her panties, but she had snuck a finger into the bottom of them. That might not be breaking her stated rule, but it would have been a no if he had asked. On the other hand, that was so much pleasure. She had brought herself off, but she had never done it as well as Greg had.

Well, Greg pretended that he wanted to talk to her. She would let him, but only talk. If he really liked her, he would stick around. Then, too, she really needed somebody to talk to just now.

Greg had a favorite story he told too often. It involved a guy who was pacing the floor after midnight. His wife asks him why he's so worried.

"I owe thousands of dollars to Sam," he says. "It's due Monday, and I don't have any way to pay it back." She says that she will solve his problem. She calls Sam.

"Sam," she says on the phone, "This is Martha, George's wife. You know that money he owes you. Well, he doesn't have it, and he can't pay you back." She hangs up the phone and turns to her husband. "Now it's Sam's problem, George. Let him worry about it. You come to bed."

Well, he'd made his case to Anne. Now it was her problem. He, however, couldn't relax and let her worry about it. For one thing, he'd been an idiot to buy condoms in Randolph. He wondered whether Copper City would have been safer, but it was another hour's drive east. Still, that was a bygone. He had already made that blunder.

The problem, as he saw it, was twofold. Her friends knew about the purchase. And he guessed that she hadn't decided whether to have sex with him. If she had decided to do so, the purchase would have been an embarrassment. She would have chided him and gone on.

If she had definitely decided to not have sex with him, she would make fun of his hopes to her friends and gone on. If she were still deciding, it would look to her both as though he had invited the town into her private thoughts and as though he were denying her the right to make that decision.

Well, he got the Jeep back Friday and got caught up in all his duties in administering the dig since he didn't have anything else to do. Sunday rolled around. He sat in the diner, and she served him his chile and his coffee. At closing time, she handed him the broom. She filled the salt and pepper shakers, and she wasn't finished by the time he had the broom away. They walked out the door together, and she locked it. She turned towards her house, not his Jeep.

"Look," he said. "I've apologized, and I apologize again for where I made my purchase. I will not apologize for what I purchased. Part of respecting your right to make decisions in those matters is my responsibility to act responsibly whatever you decide. Those don't have an expiration date. Having them doesn't mean that I expect to use them. It means that I'm prepared if I have the opportunity to use them."

"That's all water over the dam." She must have got that metaphor from reading. This part of the country didn't have enough water to need a dam. "We're not talking about that sort of thing. We're only talking, and we're talking about serious concerns." Nice of her to decide all that, and nice to tell him that he's getting frozen out of her life was not a serious concern. However, it might be that he would play her game. He wanted her, and he had to convince her that he was as interested in her as he was interested in having her body.

"Okay," he said. "I'd suggest that, if we want to talk, talking in the Jeep is better than talking standing up. Second, serious talk means more than your present problems, though you can bring them to the table when you wish. Serious talk includes what happened in your past, and tales about your roommate."

Anne had all her arguments ready, and now his agreement had destroyed their use, destroyed them. She felt as off-balance as though she had braced to lift a heavy box and found that it was empty. The only point of contention was his sudden interest in Karen. Had he figured out, as she had, that Karen would have jumped into his bed?

"What's with the concentration on Karen?" she asked. "Do you have her in your sights now that you've lost me?"

"Karen," he said with a snap in his voice, "Is the only person you've mentioned to me except your mother.... Well, you and me, but she's the only person not present whom you've discussed."

She had to admit the point of that, but she didn't have to admit it to him. They'd got to the porch and went to the door.

"And we can talk about you, too," she said as she went inside. He knew all about Karen, and she didn't even know the names of any of his friends.

Greg thought as he turned toward his Jeep that Anne was turning into the parody of the typical woman. She was mad at him, and they couldn't talk about why she was angry. They had to talk about other things. And her dictum about talk meant that she wasn't going to make out with him. Well, she was unaware of her charms. If he couldn't touch her, couldn't see most of her, he could still listen to her lovely voice. Of course, it hadn't been that lovely right then when she was so angry with him.

If they couldn't talk about it, though, she would have to talk about other subjects. Then her voice would be back to its lovely natural tone. What he would not do was tell Anne she was cute when she was angry. A guy had used that line on Diane once, and she had nearly decked him. Greg had taught Diane to punch, and he was proud of his student.

Well, Tuesday was another day, and he'd see what Anne thought then.

Anne had more worries than she could schedule. Mom's illness was first, of course, and that was entangled with the financial worries. Greg's misbehavior was an entirely separate issue, except that Greg was the only one she could talk about Mom. Then, too, Mom wanted to know about Greg. Really, Mom wanted Greg out of Anne's life. But that was her life, and she wasn't quite willing to do what Mom wanted about it.

"What are you doing about that man?" Mom asked when they were together in the Diner with no customers. That meant that Mom had stayed later on Monday than she usually did. How had Mom managed all that scolding and nagging when she was a teenager? How had she captured Anne to talk to her without customers being present?

"Greg is on a strict limit. We can talk, but we can't kiss."

"I'm not worried about kissing," Mom said.

"Well, we can't do that, either. He never tried anything else without the kissing first. He's not a grabber."

"What do you know about grabbers?"

"Honestly, Mom," Anne said. "I didn't tell you everything that happened in high school."

"So he wants to seduce you, not rape you? I should be happy about that? I want him gone, totally out of our lives."

"Well, he is doing something archeological on that mesa way west of town. We're the closest town. You can't expect them to drive to Copper City, now can you?"

"And you want to talk to him," Mom said. It wasn't a question. Yes, really, she did.

On Tuesday, he was back. They went to his Jeep after closing the diner.

"So," he said. "What is the topic of conversation?"

"How about you? What is it like to grow up in a big family?"

"What makes you think I ever did? Grow up, that is." She gave that the silence it so richly deserved. "I was the oldest kid, which is a special situation right there. I suppose there was a time when I was the only child." Rather definitely, in her opinion. "Norman was only 19 months younger, though, so I can't remember that time. You bully them; you coach them; you protect them from bullies; you argue with your parents in their favor; you complain that they get privileges that you didn't at that age.

"Then, too, Diane was a girl. I taught her to punch. She can't really box. At least, she couldn't when I knew her. As Dad would have tanned my hide if I'd landed one punch on where her tits are now, I never threw a punch at her. So she didn't know how to block anything. On the other hand, I had a punching bag, and I trained her on that. She developed a wicked left hook. One guy told her that she was cute when she was angry. She landed the left hook on him out of nowhere. Almost knocked him down.

"'What do you think you're doing?' he asked."

"'Being cute,' she answered. That was one boyfriend who she dumped fast. But Norm and I made guys aware that she was out of bounds for some games. We agreed on that, and we weren't afraid to gang up on the dude."

"So it's all right for you to do it to me," Anne pointed out, "but it's not something which should be done to your innocent sister -- an innocent sister, I might note, with a wicked left hook."

"Look, first, she was in high school. Second, what she didn't report and the guy didn't boast about wouldn't have come to our ears. Norm's ears, really. Once she was in high school, I was out of there."

"And if her current boyfriend bought a box of contraceptives in those days?"

"He'd probably have bought them in Minneapolis, and we wouldn't have heard about it. I'll bet every guy who took her out after freshman year had a condom in his wallet. All the guys did when I was in school."

"And you?" she asked.

"Well, sure. When I was in high school, I was a high school boy. When you were a baby, you couldn't walk, couldn't talk, couldn't control your bladder or bowels. You screamed for what you wanted. I don't hold that against you. I don't think it's fair to hold having been a highschool boy against me." She wasn't really holding having been a highschool boy against him. Really, he should have kept the contraceptive in his wallet instead of buying a new box.

"Well, I grew out of it sooner."

"Younger maybe," he said. "I graduated from high school twelve years ago."

"I was out of diapers long before age nine."

"Okay. I just think of myself as much older than you. Nine years isn't a lot. You're older than Ross. Now for you. What courses did you enjoy most?"

"Where do you get the idea," she asked, "that you get to pick a topic?" Still it was an intriguing question. "Most of the history courses I took are surveys. I have to be able to teach highschool courses. Last semester, though, I had space in my schedule and I took a course on plagues and how they have changed history."

"Yeah. And not always negatively. There was a great die-off in the middle ages, and that left fewer laborers for the same cleared land and the same set of tools. Wages rose, and the market power of the workers was better in lots of ways."

"You took that course?"

Greg said, "I've read a book." He could kick himself. She'd been talking about what interested her, and he had to show off. If he'd kept his mouth closed, he could have heard her speak for minutes more.

"You know," she said, "I sometimes forget that you're a professor." And he sometimes forgot that he wasn't in front of a lecture hall.

"That's the nicest thing you've said about me in a week." She smiled at that.

"No. I like professors. Why don't you drive me back, now?" He started the Jeep.

"Why don't you make a list of my good points and my bad points sometime tomorrow when there are no customers," he suggested. "That way you could give them to me and I'll work on keeping the good points up front."

"And you'll do the same for me?"

"Sure, if I can think of any bad points." He let her out close to her door. He didn't see the point of walking her there, but he did wait until she was inside.

"Did you make the list?" Anne asked him when they were alone in the diner Thursday.

"Yes, did you? I'll trade." She gave him a paper, and he gave her one. He put hers in his shirt pocket while he swept. She read his sitting at a table.

"You're sweet," she said.

His list had gone:
Pretty
  Face
  Skin
  Hair
  ( )
  ] [
  ( )
  Voice
Smart
Responsible
Vivacious
Caring
Hard worker

His only negative was:
Blames herself for what life does to her.

"Open mine," she said.

Her list said:
+Intelligent
+Educated
+Strong
+Can take no for an answer
+Empathetic
+Acknowledges his mistakes

-Can do the dumbest things
-Lustful
-Sneaky
-Stubborn

"Well," he said, "Six positives and four negatives. Does that make me a good guy? And if by 'lustful' you mean that I desire you, that only makes me a guy. I'll bet that, when you walk down the hall in school, most of the guys you pass look at you with desire."

"If so, they don't show it as obviously as you do. What are those parenthetical expressions?"

"Those are the parts of you that I'm not supposed to discuss right now."

"Then, they are the parts you aren't supposed to mention ever again.... Which parts?"

He laughed. "You can't have it both ways. Did I forget to mention that you are curious? Well, I said intelligent and curious is one aspect. As for the other question, two are from a front view, and the other one is what can be seen from behind."

Anne said, "And you deny that you are lustful! That's too mild a word. You're a dirty old man." The truth was, however, that she didn't mind his suggesting that she was sexually attractive so long as he wasn't obnoxious about it. Teasing was fine. She should have listed a sense of humor among his positives. She went to put the dishes through the dishwasher. This was a restaurant model with continuous feed. When the place was clean, she locked up and headed home.

"We had our discussion already?" he asked. He was walking along.

"Yeah." She almost stopped for a good-night kiss at the door. Then she remembered that she was depriving him. The problem was, she was depriving herself, too.

Greg noted her hesitation. He went back to his Jeep happy. The next time would be Saturday. The list, on the other hand, hasn't been too helpful. "Can do the dumbest things" really meant that he had done the dumbest thing -- the dumbest single thing in the history of stupidity. Even if he refrained from more stupidity, he wouldn't become the guy who hadn't done that. He was lustful because other guys hid it better, and he was sneaky. You could work on one of those, but both were a stretch. And he had to admit he was stubborn, but he wasn't going to win this gal by being less stubborn.

Saturday, they sat in his Jeep and talked about general things. The next day, however, he got a kiss for driving her home.

The next Saturday, they sat in the Jeep and kissed. He kept his hands on her shoulders and above, mostly by running them through her hair.

The Saturday after that, they went out into the country again. She specified that she would stay dressed. He lay on his back on the blanket and lifted her above him. They kissed, and he stroked her. He didn't remove one piece of clothing, but he spent a long time kneading her rump. He started worrying about the calendar, though. The dig would only last through the summer.

That Tuesday, she told him about the new problems her mother's tests had shown. The last operation hasn't got it all, and it had metastasized into the liver. She went a hundred miles each way for radiation, and she took a chemo cocktail at home. He wasn't going to mention the looming closing of the dig. It wasn't a problem to compare to hers. They didn't cover any new ground Thursday. When she repeated the Tuesday list, however, she did so with less desperation in her voice.

Saturday, he was prepared to talk. She was going through Hell, and he wasn't going to add to it. Instead of talking, she wanted to go watch the stars again. There, she peeled down to her panties. He still had the Trojans in the glove compartment, but he didn't carry the single in his pocket anymore. Maybe he should. All he took off, though, were his shirt, his shoes, and his socks. She looked beautiful in the starlight, and he said so.

Anne didn't want to be told she was beautiful. She didn't want to be loved, even. She wanted to be excited until she forgot, and Greg was the most excitement that she had ever had. He kissed her in a loving fashion at first, deep kisses which were exciting, and then small kisses all over her face which didn't arouse as much. When he started down her neck, she couldn't wait any longer. She grabbed his head and moved his lips to her nipple. Now, that was exciting. He moved from one nipple to the other, and his hand went to her delta.

When his finger went inside her panties to explore the folds there, she spreads her legs wide and pushed her mound up to get more stimulation from the finger. When it found her clit, she clasped her hand over it to hold it right there.

"Yes," she said when she went over. She shook, and her arms and legs jumped around.

He sucked hard on the nipple, and it hurt. She needed that hurt, though. He stroked her clit again, and she wanted more. She shook again, and it was very good.

When she couldn't move any more, he took his finger out of the panties and lay beside her. She was sweating and shivering, and he put her skirt over her legs and his shirt over her top. He lay beside her with an arm over her stomach.

Greg didn't know how much later it was when he woke up, but the stars above them had moved. He got her up, dressed, and in the Jeep. He tossed the blanket in the back and put his shoes and socks on. He drove her home. Only when she got out of the Jeep did he take his shirt back. He led her to the door.

"I love you," he said. She didn't respond, and he didn't think she heard him. He'd been loud enough, but she looked mostly asleep.

Sunday, though, she looked rested. They talked some more. She didn't have any changes to report, but she spoke more positively about the future. When she seemed to have talked as much as she needed to, he kissed her. They spent the last ten minutes with his tongue chasing hers and his hands tangled in her hair.

Anne had heard quite clearly what Greg had said, Saturday. She was mostly asleep, but she thought that she would have heard those three words if she were dead when he said them. He didn't repeat them Sunday, but he acted as if they were true.

They sat in the diner after they had cleaned up. He heard her lay out all her worries and hopes. They kissed, and she felt that the world was good. That feeling lasted for the walk home, and for the last kiss of the night -- the kiss in the doorway. Then she went in and closed the door on him, on pleasure, on hope.

She knew he would be coming Tuesday, though, and that carried her through the next two days. He sat at the counter Tuesday night. He ate chile and drank coffee. When she had closed up and they had cleaned the place, they came together. They kissed and made out. When he sat on a stool, She stood between his knees with her back to him. He kissed her neck and held her breasts. She let all the tensions and worries of the two days flow out her back and into his chest and all the pleasure he provided flow from his hands into her breasts. When she was empty of tension and full of pleasure, he walked her home. She leaned on him as she went, and he supported her with his strength.

Wednesday, she talked to the empty diner just as though he had been there. She told him that she loved him. She told him that she wanted him. She wouldn't have dared if he had been there. Thursday, they talked.

Really, she talked and he listened. Somehow, her fears eased when she told them to him, while they just got worse when she told them to an empty diner. He walked her home, and their kiss at the door was hotter than ever. She would have invited him in if she had been certain that Mom wouldn't wake up.

Friday and Saturday were walking over hot coals with no other help than the promise that he would come.

"Do you want to talk more?" he asked when they'd cleaned up Saturday night.

"Not here." So he drove them to a spot out away from the road. They kissed once before leaving the Jeep. Lying beside each other on the blanket, they kissed again. She led his hands to the buttons on her blouse. She rolled away so he could get the bra straps, then rolled towards him so she could unbutton his shirt. Then they were kissing again, with her nipples feeling his chest hair around them. She was hot where he was touching her, and cold where he had touched her and moved on. She stopped tasting chile in his kiss, and tasted only him and wanting.

He rolled her over on her back, and he kissed down to her breasts. His lips and tongue drew a line of fire from her neck to her nipple. It was so hard that it hurt before he sucked it. When he asked her to raise herself so he could remove her skirt, she shoved up so far that her hips were as high as her knees.

He kissed down over her stomach to the waist of her panties. This time, she raised herself before he even asked. When the panties were around her knees, she took them off herself. His kisses went back to her breasts, and this time it was the right nipple's time to feel like it was burning. He kissed the inside of her right thigh, and desire flowed from his lips to her center.

His lips followed, slowly. He couldn't kiss her there, but he did, and she couldn't say no to him. He licked the folds, and she raised her hips off the ground again. He got her hips in his hands and raised her to his mouth. When his tongue found her clitoris, she was helpless. She felt warmth spread from his mouth into her stomach and then all through her body. Her hands grabbed his hair to hold him there, and she wriggled helplessly as the warmth spread.

Then fire shot out of her center into her entire body. She writhed and moaned. She was all tension, every muscle pulling her against all the others. Then she was nothing, a limp dishrag. He let his hands down on the blanket. She could feel that her hips were pressing them against the ground.

"Never," she said when she could catch her breath. "Never, ever. Nobody could do that."

"Your first kiss like that?" he asked.

"First," she said. This was the first time she had even had her panties off with a boy.

"Second," he said. And, with no more warning, he was kissing her there again.

Greg was damned proud he'd given Anne a pleasure nobody else had given her. Between her time restrictions and his blunder about buying condoms in her home town, their time was running out. He could no longer brand her as his with the length of their affair. He would make sure that she remembered this night. He started in again, trying to extract from her the most pleasure she could possibly experience. He teased her with his tongue. He squeezed her butt cheeks while he licked her labia. He went on to her clitoris.

When she was moving as though she were close, he left her clit for another session with her labia. When she pushed her mound up into his mouth, he went back to long licks finishing on her clitoris. When she finally went over with groans and writhings, he sucked directly over her clit until she stopped.

Anne had never felt anything remotely like this. She had had dreams, and had learned to please herself. Nothing she had experienced, however, had been anything like the first one. And this one was the first one doubled and prolonged. When she collapsed, Greg pulled his hands out from under her hips. He moved up beside her.

"Anne," he said. "Beautiful Anne, wonderful Anne, delightful Anne." When her breathing slowed, she turned her head toward him. He kissed her. She tasted something different, and not too pleasant.

"Is that me?"

"Yeah. I don't think it's supposed to taste as good to women."

"You're wonderful to me," she said. Were they going to make love now? She didn't feel as eager as she had felt some minutes ago, but he had been wonderful to her, and she was totally naked and open to him. Would he stop if she asked now? Would she ask him to stop now?

Greg said, "You're beautiful." He got up on one elbow to look at her. She was ethereal in the moonlight, but fairly clearly delineated. Only the secrets between her legs were hidden. She looked damned sexy lying like this, looked like she was satiated. Admittedly, she had been even sexier in the throes of her climax. He hadn't had much of a view then, and this view was going on much longer. He bent over to kiss her breastbone while his face enjoyed a breast brushing either side of it.

When he pulled back, she rolled over on her side. This was another view, with much deeper shadows. Then the edge of her body, though, from half-way down her rib cage to her ankle was highlighted by the moonlight. Her femininity was emphasized; her waist bent in incredibly deep, and her hip was thrown far up because her other one was lying flat against the ground. From the raised hip to just above the knee was one smooth curve.

"You're beautiful," he repeated.

"You're prejudiced."

"Maybe. I don't want to show this sight to any other man to get a second judgment." He didn't think he was prejudiced though, or -- if he were -- that this meant that she didn't have great beauty.

Anne thought he sounded awfully possessive. She wasn't about to complain, though. She liked thinking of herself as Greg's possession. Which was strange, since she had kicked so hard against Mom's thinking of her as Molly's daughter when she so wanted to be her own woman. Of course, she was her own woman now, a woman with a mother to take care of, and that wasn't what you would call fun.

When she thought of Greg's possessing her, though, she thought of sex. They had come awfully close. Accepting what he had just done meant that she really didn't have any excuse to deny him the rest, did she? Mom said not until marriage, and Greg hadn't even mentioned marriage. Karen said it was okay if you were in love, and Greg had said that he loved her. She certainly loved Greg. She did think that Greg should ask her. She didn't want him to try to force her against her will, but he could be more forceful. A girl didn't offer to give a guy her virginity; he persuaded her. She thought about that and shivered.

Greg saw the shiver. "Cold?" he asked. The sight was delightful, but he didn't want her getting sick from this. He moved over her for a deep kiss. This was much more comfortable than standing, and he felt all of her against almost all of him. Then, too, he was shielding her from the desert breeze. What he wasn't shielding her from was his erection. It tried to get through his khakis and into her. Well, it didn't succeed, but this was probably time to get dressed and get her back.

"Should we return you home?" he asked.

"Should, yes. But it's so nice here." Nevertheless, when he got off her, she got up on hands and knees and started gathering her clothes. The view from behind which this afforded was so arousing that his cock hurt. He kept looking, though.

Soon, she was nearly dressed. He put his shirt and shoes back on. By then she was in the Jeep. He got the blanket into the Jeep and took them back to town. At her door, he crushed her to him. His kiss was hungry, and hers was yielding. He watched her go in and stared at the closed door for a minute. Then he got back in the Jeep and headed out to the mesa. He still had the box of Trojans in the glove compartment, but he thought he should get one of them into his pocket before he visited the diner next Saturday.

This business of yielding to the hours the diner was open was frustrating. But Anne was a product of the diner. The diner had supported her for decades. She was loyal to her mother, yes. But she was loyal to that work pattern, too. And, if you really wanted a woman, you especially wanted her to be loyal.

Anne went to bed remembering the heated kiss at the end. She remembered his erection pressing against her when he lay on her. His words weren't demanding, but his body certainly was. Well, she had a week to dream about it and consider it, but she knew her answer if he asked her next Saturday.

Sunday, they talked a little. Then they kissed a lot. Tuesday, they didn't talk much, but they made out in the diner. "Saturday," she whispered to him when he let her go after the last kiss at her door. By Thursday, Mom was feeling worse. She laid out her troubles and fears after they'd cleaned out the diner. She sat on his lap and cried. They didn't have much time to make out then, but he whispered "Saturday" to her before the last kiss at her door. She whispered "Saturday" to him after he let her go. She consciously wiggled her hips as she walked through the door.

Friday, Mom wasn't much help at breakfast. When it was time for her to come over to help with the lunch crowd, she didn't show up. When the last of them had been fed, she called on her cell.

"I'm not feeling well," Mom said. She hadn't been feeling well for months, and she'd admitted it since Anne had got back from school. Still, the weak, quavering voice frightened Anne. She cleared the dishes as soon as people looked done. The customers got the hint, and they started eating faster. As soon as the last one left, she locked the door and ran to the house. Mom looked like she was already dead. She called Dr. Green, Mom's doctor. He told her to bring Mom in.

Anne was able to get her to her car and to Dr. Green's office in Copper City. The office nurse took one look when she came in, and took Mom's blood pressure. When the doctor came out of the examining room, he and the nurse had a hurried, whispered conference. He helped Mom into the other examining room. The people with appointments sitting in the waiting room looked more worried about Mom than they did about having to wait. After an examination and an attempt to ask Mom questions, Dr. Green went to the phone to call for an ambulance to take Mom to the hospital.

When the ambulance came, the attendants took Mom away, and the doctor said something about plasma. She could do nothing, so she went back to the car and drove home. She opened the diner for supper, but she closed early and called the hospital. Mom was resting easy, and she was over the crisis. That was the same hospital where they had done the last surgery, and Dr. Green knew the surgeon and the guy who did the radiation. There was nothing that Anne could do except talk to Mom, and she wasn't talking much. There was even less that Greg could do, but she wished he were there to talk to.

Saturday, she put in a full day in the diner. Greg came in, and took one look at her. She thought she'd been hiding it well, but he took his hamburger and coffee and sat at a table on the far side of the room. When the last other customer left, a few minutes after 9:30, he came over.

"What happened?" he asked. She must have stumbled, because he grabbed her and held her up.

"Mom. She's in the hospital. She's much worse." He sat down and lifted her onto his lap.

"Cry," he said. He patted his shoulder.

"I c-can't." And then she did. He held her with one arm and patted her shoulder with the other.

"You've kept the place open?" he asked.

"I closed it for a couple hours to get her to the doctor's office. She wasn't bad Thursday, not healthy, but no worse than usual. Then, Friday morning, she wasn't much help with the breakfast crowd. Then, at noon, she couldn't get here. When I next saw her, she looked like an Egyptian mummy. I got her to the doctor, and he got her to the hospital. They sent an ambulance. I don't know."

"You know, I've never met her, but I understand how she operates. That's 'cause you go like that, and you have to get it from somewhere. She goes as long as there is anything in the tank. Then she can't go any longer. People I know, they'd put a sign on the diner: 'Closed -- Molly's sick.' You two don't act like that."

"Well, I'll get to the hospital tomorrow," she said. "We open late on Sunday."

"The diner starts at noon. Anne starts at dawn."

"Pretty much. I'm sorry. I promised you so much."

"Look," he said. "I may be a selfish brute, but not even I am that selfish. I'd suggest locking the doors and walking you home right now, but I know you don't operate like that. Where is the broom?" So they cleaned up. "What hospital?" he asked.

"St. Catherine's in Flagstaff," she said. He walked her home and folded her in his arms. She shook, and he just held her instead of kissing her. She noticed, though, that he had an erection. After he'd left, she managed to get completely undressed before falling into bed. Somehow, she fell right asleep.

In the morning, she took the drive to the hospital.

"What happened to the diner?" Mom asked when she got to her room.

"Mom, it's Sunday morning. The diner is always closed on Sunday mornings. I'll open it at noon as always."

"I used to have life insurance. I spent most of it on tuition. Why would you need life insurance if you were going to be making your own living. Now, your only support is the diner. It's all I can leave you."

"I know, Mom." She also knew that there were serious bills. Mom had medical insurance, but there was a co-pay.

"It was my life. I poured everything into making your life possible. And I failed."

"You didn't fail, Mom. I'm here. The diner is here, well there."

"But you won't be a teacher." Mom was probably right.

"Well, I don't know," Anne said. "After all, I got through three years. If I have to go to night school or something, I'm way ahead of where I would be without that."

"You can't work the diner and go to school. There isn't any college within a hundred miles of Randolph. You're thinking of selling the diner? I looked at the market. We owe more on it than we could sell it for."

"Well, you supported yourself and me with the diner. If I have to, I can support myself."

"Well," Mom said, "you can as long as you don't fall for a man. Don't let that guy seduce you."

"You worry too much about that. Just concentrate on getting well."

"Getting well? Hmpf!" That was the last Mom said, and soon she was back asleep. Anne stayed by her too long, and then went back. She had miscalculated, and she got back to Randolph at 12:23. There were two couples and a loner waiting in their cars. When she had unlocked, they came in. Both women asked after Mom. They settled down at tables and waited until she was ready. Nobody mentioned the wait, and there were tips on all those tables when she cleared them. Before they went out, more people came in.

***

Greg got away from the Mesa at a few minutes before 2:00 on Sunday. Google got him a route to the hospital, and he followed it. The sun was still in the sky when he got there, and visiting hours weren't over.

He knocked on the doorframe of Mrs. Bernard's room. She looked in his direction, and he went in.

"Mrs. Bernard? I'm Eric Thibault. I'm a friend of your daughter's."

"A friend? Is that what you call it?" Well, she knew who he was, then. "Why are you here?" Now that was a good question. He didn't really know. Anne's mother was the center of her life. He wanted to be the center of Anne's life.

"Well," he said. "You're very important to her, and she's very important to me. That makes you important to me."

"You're trying to ruin her."

"The last thing I'd want would be to damage her."

"You bought those things to ruin her," she said.

"Well, I bought condoms in Randolph. That embarrassed her, and I've apologized. I apologize to you, too. It probably embarrassed you more. After all, those are all your friends and neighbors who've heard the gossip. In my defense, I'm a city guy, and I'm not used to purchases being gossiped about."

"I don't want her making my mistakes."

"Children don't, you know. They make their own mistakes. We all make our own decisions. Some of them, a fairly large percentage, are mistakes. But you can't avoid making decisions, and there is no way to know in advance which decision is right."

"You want to put a child into her," she said, "and leave her like I was left." Now that was interesting. Hadn't Anne said that her father died when she was very young? Molly seemed to be saying that Anne's dad had simply run away. Did everybody who knew Anne but him know that?

"No. Neither one, really. If all that you know about me is that I bought some condoms, then you should figure out that I don't want to make Anne pregnant. And, I'm not at all interested in leaving her. Physically, of course. I'm done out on Long Mesa soon, and I'm going back to being an assistant professor at the University of Colorado. I wrote out some contact information." He put the sheet on the sort of cabinet by her bed. "I'll give them to her before I leave town.

"Unfortunately," he continued, "the contact information doesn't work too well right now. The cell phone connection is very bad out at the mesa. That is why I came into your diner in the first place. The e-mail account will send back a notice that I'm out of touch and then delete your message. Clearly, I'm neither at the apartment, nor in my office. Still, it is long-term contact information. I'm not going to disappear."

"Says you."

"Says me. Look, Anne and I may be in the same relationship. We are, however, in very different positions. I'm newly a director of a dig with grad students as my subordinates. It's not the pinnacle of my career, at least I hope not. Still, it is a solid beginning. Anne is under enormous stress.

"So, I've seen her at her worst, and I like what I see, and I'm in a good position to judge. Anne has seen me near my best, and she is under too much strain to judge. She has been comfortable talking to me, but she would have been comforted by talking to anybody right now. I like what I see, and that is almost certain to continue. If Anne likes what she sees, and I have good reason to believe that she does, nobody has any reason to believe that this liking will continue when the stress is removed.

"So, I want to keep connected. Whether that connection will bear fruit is Anne's decision."

"You mean after I'm dead," she said.

"Um..." He'd been trying like hell to avoid saying that.

"Everybody dances around that. Well, I love Anne, and I won't force her to say it. I have no reason at all to love you. I'm dying. Now, say it."

"You're dying. I don't know how soon; I'm not a medical doctor."

"Damn soon. At some point there'll be more cancer in this body than there is me. Well, you may think that you'll win then, but I'll protect Anne as long as I'm above ground. Now, go away. I'm ringing the bell, and I'll tell them that you're tiring me."

"You know, attaching to me might be the greatest mistake in her life," he started.

"Well, you admit it."

"And not attaching to me might be. I don't know any way to decide beforehand. Goodbye," As he walked out, a nurse was coming towards the room. In the Jeep, he found out that Long Mesa wasn't on Google Maps. He asked directions to Randolph though he hadn't come through there on the way. He knew how to get back from there.

Mrs. Bernard's question was still a good one. You could take it as a given that he hadn't accomplished anything by that visit. What was less clear was what he'd thought he could accomplish. At some point in a romance, the girl brought you home to meet her family. He had only got that far once, and that once had been as an undergraduate. Had he tried to pre-empt Anne on that? Well, was Anne at that point in their relationship? He clearly was. And the family had rejected him.

Anne had not taken him to meet Molly simply because she knew that he'd be rejected? Was it the situation? Hell! Anne spent her waking hours in the diner. He'd cut down the time they had together since she needed some other time. Anne certainly spoke to Molly. (Somehow, he thought of her in that way. Was it that she put her name on the diner? He'd known her name before he'd known Anne's.) She could have brought him along on one of those times. Or was Molly in bed when they spoke. Molly spent some time in the diner; was that when they talked? If he had come at noon, would he have met Molly? Well, Anne never suggested that.

He'd told Molly that he and Anne were in the same relationship, but were they really? He was having real uncertainty about marriage with Anne. Was Anne even considering him for marriage?

His parents had been married for more than 25 years when they were killed together in a car crash. He thought of marriage as lasting the rest of your life. He didn't doubt that he wanted a marriage with Anne --

wanted to spend the rest of his life married to Anne. What he doubted was that they were in a situation to really make such a commitment. And that was a doubt that Anne was in that situation.

As he'd told her mother, he had seen Anne deal with horrible tension. She had a lovely face and a lovely body, sure. She was ethereal by starlight, and he really wanted to see her body in better light. But that body and that voice, were only icing on the cake of her spirit. Life had kicked her, and she'd come back. Hell! She had worked in the diner since high school. He'd known kids who worked for their pocket money and bitched like hell about it. She had worked so hard that college was a break, and then she'd come back from college to be ground down. What was full-time work? Forty hours a week? She worked two full-time jobs, and more.

At a dig, the hours were closer to 60 a week. If, however, someone broke to drink water or took a long lunch, nobody bitched. Anne had to schedule her meals and her John breaks around when customers were in the diner. She slaved away, and she did it because her mother, all the family she had ever known, was sick and dying.

He wanted to take Anne away from all that. He wanted to help her finish school. Sure, he wanted to enjoy her body while he did, but she would cook for only him and herself. (Well, he had entertained the idea of her accompanying him on digs and running the kitchen, with students assigned to assist. But, really, this was his idea of an excuse to bring her along.) If she closed the diner to go see her mother in the hospital, that meant less money to pay the hospital bills. She could have a job; she wanted to teach. But never again would a job have her; never again would she have to go to work every day or have nowhere to sleep that night.

But he was afraid of offering her that. First of all, she was at a damned bad time for considering anything. He was doing her best by listening to her concerns and doing her more good, even, by diverting her from her concerns. Not that their make-out sessions were pure acts of charity on his part; he'd wanted her from the moment he saw her, because earlier he'd heard her sexy voice before he'd seen her clearly. Still, as a diversion, he was an improvement in her life, maybe a necessity in her life. As one more life decision, he could be the breaking point. Even if she didn't break, and it seemed to him that she was the strongest person he had ever met, it would be one more burden. His idiotic shopping in Randolph had caused her worry. He didn't want to cause her any more, let alone a million times as much.

Then, too, she might see that escape from her impossible situation and take it. He wanted to take her away from all that, but he did not want her to accept him because he was her escape from all that. His parents had been married for more than 25 years. If they weren't passionate when he knew them, they were still very loving. (And how sure was he about the passion? They hadn't found Ross under a cabbage leaf.) "They wouldn't have wanted to leave you, but they would have been glad that they went together." That was almost a mantra among his parents' friends.

He wanted Anne to love him, and then for her to take the escape as a bonus. And there was no way for him to know that she did. There was probably no way for her to know it herself. She was clear-eyed. She could possibly make the decision conscious that she was doing that. On the other hand, if she thought she loved him, that thought might come as a result of the pressure.

And, on the other hand, she might say no. (On the other hand? On the third hand? This situation had more sides than one of those statues of Shiva could hold in its hands.) She had not taken him home to her family. There were alternative explanations. Maybe she didn't see any time when her mother was available. Maybe she didn't see any time when Greg and her mother were both available. Maybe she didn't want to show him her mother's weakness; she thought of her as strong, and that weakness hurt her. Maybe she didn't want to show her mother, her chance of a future when her mother had none. Showing the boy to the family is a step before engagement, an unstated exhibition of a possible future. That would have been damned awkward presentation of a woman whose future could be measured in months. Maybe she'd planned it before he'd made the damned purchase; after all, they hadn't been that far along, then, and she couldn't have foreseen how he would step in it.

And, just maybe, she never brought him home because she didn't see him like that at all. It was a summertime romance. Shit! How many guys were available for maybe half an hour after 10:00 with more on Saturdays? It had been the only summer romance on offer, and she hadn't gone all that far. He'd picture her reluctance to shed her panties, her hesitation to have sex with him, as a modest girl's slowly extending her limits. She had never claimed that, and he had never asked. He might be a boor, and after the trip to the drug store in Randolph, the "might" was only a courtesy. He wasn't enough of a boor to ask a girl about her previous experience. And, if a boor did, the girl had every right to lie. Sex was something a good girl didn't do, and when she did, it was because the guy was special. You didn't ask how many had been that special before, even when it was a one-archeological-dig affair, even when the girl had brought along a supply of pills. You certainly didn't when the girl hadn't actually put out for you.

So, Anne was special in his life. In some ways, he was special in hers. He was the only person with whom she could talk about her experience with her mother. But that might mean that there were a dozen guys whom she liked more with whom she had a long history, who also knew her mother. And, since they knew her mother, she couldn't talk to them about Molly. For that matter, her worries about the diner weren't something she wanted to share with the customer base. He was isolated from the gossip circles, and they were vicious -- as he had learned to his sorrow. So he was her favorite confidante partially, at least, because he was her only possible confidante.

But was he special in her life the way he wanted to be? Did she feel about him the way he felt about her?

And, of course, she might say no simply because she saw the advantages. If he, who trusted her so much, didn't trust her response to him to come from love instead of from desperation, then she, who mistrusted herself so unreasonably, who saw herself as weak because she shook under a load which would crush anybody else, would be likely to doubt that her response came from love.

If he proposed, she might accept him for the wrong reasons, and she might refuse him for the wrong reason. Of course, this was the utterly wrong time in her life to propose, anyway. That was the one saving grace. On the other hand (Was he up to six hands now?) it wasn't only a time in her life, it was a time in his life, too. The dig was about to close, and he was going back to Boulder. You couldn't take an extra week after the beginning of the academic year just because your life was at a critical point.

Hell! He was living on Long Mesa. Was there even a motel near Randolph? He went over the ground, he'd covered before for the rest of the trip. He didn't get any clearer, though. He got to Randolph about 8:30. If he wanted to see Anne -- well, he did want to see Anne -- driving out to the Mesa and turning around when he got there would make him too late. He didn't know anywhere else that was open. He went to the diner. He could watch her and listen to her for the next hour if not speak to her. Besides, he was actually hungry.

He got two burgers, a bowl of chile, and a cup of coffee. He sat at the counter so he could watch her bustle around and listen to her talk to the regulars. She finally came over to talk to him.

"I can't get off any earlier," she said.

"I was in town, and the drive out to the mesa and back was too long. Anyway, this is my first food since lunch."

"What have you been doing, on a Sunday and all?"

"We'll talk later," he said, "but I went to visit your mother."

"And how was she?"

"Feisty."

"Well," she said, "that means she's still alive. Other than that, she's always been feisty. Even so, I'm not sure. Maybe she'll go on being feisty." She had tears in her eyes, and she went to scrape the grill until somebody else asked for coffee.

When she closed up the place, the people going out expressed sympathy.

"Come to the table," she said. He brought his cup over, and she got one of her own and the pot. "I misjudged the time, and got here late," she said. "There were five people waiting for lunch, and all they said was to ask about her. Nobody so much as looked at his watch. I used to hate this town, but they can be nice people."

"Hate the town? I thought they were all your friends."

"They were customers. They gossiped about Mom, and they gossiped about me, the ones young enough to care. I had some girlfriends, especially in grade school. I had some boyfriends in high school, but some of them were just looking for an easy feel, and they hated me when they didn't get it. And any boy who wasn't, and I had two or three who really liked me, I thought. Well, whatever I thought, all their friends thought they were out for an easy feel. And the girls who hadn't been special friends hated me 'cause they thought the boys could get more from me."

"So, you aren't terribly attached to Randolph?" This was an important question for him. He couldn't offer her a life with him in this town. Even spending many later summers on Long Mesa would put a crimp in his career. Heading the dig this year was a step ahead for an assistant professor. Coming back next year would be nice. Coming back every successive year would be a dead end. That site had only so much to say.

"Socially? No. I have more friends in Tempe, and I've only lived there for three years. Economically? Riveted in place. I have one place to live and one place to work, and they are both here. Speaking of work..." She handed him the broom, and he began to sweep out as she took care of the dishes.

Anne left the cups and pot for last. She figured that they would be talking some more. She had really distracted herself from the big question. Why had he gone to the hospital? What had Mom thought? What, for that matter, had he thought of Mom? He got done before she did.

"You want these?" he asked, holding up the coffee stuff.

"No. I thought we might want more."

"Okay." He waited there until she came back.

"What did you think of Mom?" she asked. His word "feisty" was a perfect description of the woman she had known all her life. It sounded more like Mom than the woman who had dropped asleep in the middle of their conversation.

"How tall is she -- was she when she was healthy?" Now, that was an odd question.

"Five-five. Maybe up to my nose."

"She looked very small lying there," he said. "Your past descriptions made me think that she was a big woman."

"Well, she was a strong woman. And, after all, she was bigger than I was for most of my life."

"She's still a strong woman, probably not physically now. She handled me, and that's not so easy to do from lying down in bed." She thought that he was closest to easy to handle when she'd been lying down on a blanket. But that wasn't what he'd meant at all.

"Why did you go?" she asked.

"She asked me the same question, and I asked myself the question afterwards. I didn't have a good answer. I told her that it was because you're very important to me and she is very important to you. That makes her important to me. Does that make sense?"

"A little." And hearing that she was very important to him was one silver lining in the huge black cloud.

"Well, I'm glad," he said, "and all of that is true. It's the truth and nothing but the truth. I very much doubt that it's the whole truth....

"Look, I gave you my e-mail a long time ago." His voice told her that he was aware that he was changing the subject.

"Yeah." And she had it hidden away where she couldn't lose it.

"And if you sent me an e-mail there today, the program would send back a response saying that I was away from my desk until September 16. Then the program would dump your e-mail. I gave your mother several pieces of contact information long-term. All that I have with me is my cell phone, and that is problematical when I'm on the mesa. I do check voicemail occasionally, though. Generally, these days, when I'm available for communication, I'm on my way to see you. That doesn't help you very much."

"Unless, I want to tell you to stay away," she said. She never did, though.

"Which is why I never gave you my cell number. Well, before the dig closes, I'll give it to you and a couple of other contact numbers."

"'The dig closes'? When will that be?" He hadn't spoken of this before.

"About September eighth. I may be up there for a few days more, maybe some others will stay with me. These aren't all Colorado students, and some of them leave earlier. Some have already gone."

"So, we are about to come to the end of our time?" He didn't ever get to use any of those rubbers. Was he sorry that he'd spent so much time on her? And, if so, why did he go visit Mom?

"No! Well, this association is about to end. I'm not going to come into the diner and sweep up for you in October. What I'm talking about is keeping some association. I want to talk to you and, maybe, send you letters. I want to keep in touch and know how it goes with your mother. I want to hear how you are bearing up."

He made it sound as though he were interested in more than her body.

"I'm sure that there are prettier girls in Boulder."

"So, when you come to Boulder, wear your hair down."

"What?" And when did her coming to Boulder become something possible?

"You have a lovely face and a lovely body," he said. "You also have absolutely gorgeous hair. If you think you have competition in boulder, wear your hair down, and you'll be certain to overshadow them even more. That bun is as concealing as the apron."

She went to hang up her apron. As she came back, she pulled the pins out of her hair. When she got to the table, he got up. They flowed together in a kiss. His lips and his tongue thrilled her, he pulled her close and then ran his hands through her hair. It was wonderful; it was peace after all the pain. And, when she thought that, the pain came back. Tears sprang out of her eyes. She left his mouth to burrow into his chest and sob. He held her close and patted her back.

"I'm sorry," she sobbed.

"Why? You have damned good reason to cry. And when you need to cry, my shoulder is always available to cry on." Minutes later, when the flood of tears was drying off, he asked, "Do you want me to walk you home?"

"Please." They left the cups and pot sitting on the table, probably the first time for Molly's diner since it had opened twenty years before. When they got to her door, he kissed her forehead. She hid her tears until she was inside with the door closed.

Everything was going wrong. Mom was dying. She had known it all summer, but now it was coming closer. Greg, her only support, was going back to his school. And she would never go back to hers.

Tuesday, she managed to smile sweetly to the last customers to leave at 10:00. She was getting more traffic now, and more of them were leaving tips. It was almost as if people were showing support in the only way that they could. Still, she wished that they would leave earlier. Greg held her and kissed her forehead again.

After a little crying, she straightened up. They cleaned up the diner, and he walked her home.

"Look," he said on the way. "I set the Sunday, Tuesday, Thursday, Saturday schedule because I thought you needed your sleep. Do you want me to change it? Do you want more days? Fewer days?"

"No. Yes... I don't know."

"Well, as I told you long ago, I can do as you decide, but I can't decide as you would decide."

"Well, I want you all the time. I don't want to run the diner. I just want to hide in your arms and cry.... But I can't. Why don't we stick to the schedule we have. Of course, Saturday night..."

"Saturday night," he said, "is no longer the night before you can sleep in. Therefore, we can't enjoy it the way we used to.... You did enjoy it, didn't you?"

"Yes, very much. It couldn't have been too enjoyable for you."

"Anne, really. Those Saturdays were, some of them were, the high points of my year."

They had reached her door. He kissed her forehead, but she wouldn't allow that. She grabbed his head and pulled him into a real kiss. Her lips pressed against his, but it was his tongue which explored her mouth.

She kept working with brief calls to Mom or the hospital when the traffic in the diner slowed down. She was jittery on Thursday evening, anxious about his arrival. When he came in, the anxiety eased, and all that bothered her was the customers remaining. They trickled out and all left by 10:00. She came into his arms. This was more for comfort than for making out, and he always seemed to know the difference.

"Look," he said when she left the sanctuary of his arms. "I said I'd give you contact info for later. Here it is." He took an index card out of his pocket and gave it to her. "The top e-mail is personal. The second is my academic account at the University. Basically, the first one is the one to use, but you can always copy to the second one. Similarly, the first number is my cell, and despite current problems, is probably the one to use. I don't answer it when I'm in class, but I check voicemail and messages fairly often. The next two are my apartment and my office land lines. The last is the department. If I'm incommunicado, they should, at least know why. If you call them, you're dealing with a bureaucracy, and a bureaucracy that isn't interested in helping you. But, if you get desperate, they are there."

"So, if I'm not supposed to call them," she asked, "why did you give me that number?"

"Well, two reasons. I can imagine your calling and I'm stuck in some conference in some other city. Still, I should get voice mail. The other thing is that I realized -- realized when I was talking with your mother, as a matter of fact -- that you only have my word for it that I'm with the University at all. I doubt that she's convinced." She had never doubted that he taught college. She'd decided that he talked like a professor before he had said that he was. Whatever her doubts about him, they had never extended to his being a professor.

"I'm convinced."

"Want to see my faculty ID?" he asked.

"I'd love to see it. I believe you, but I'd love to see your ID." He got it out of his wallet. When he did, he also passed her his driver's license, voter's registration card, library card, and three credit cards. The faculty card had a picture of him in coat and tie and with a much shorter haircut. When you looked at details, it was Greg's face. The general impression was not Greg at all. It was his stuffy, dull twin. The driver's license had him with an open collar, at least, but looking much younger.

"Now, I don't believe you. I said you sounded like a professor, but you didn't look like one. You certainly don't look like that professor."

"Sorry about that. Want me to sweep the floor?" And so he did. When they walked back, she told him about her calls and how little she could find out about Mom's condition at this distance. The conversation took longer than the walk. Finally, he said, "Well, what's real in this situation? You know the prognosis, and you tell me she looked comparatively healthy the day before her collapse. If you were there, would seeing her tell you more than seeing her told you then?"

"You're not much comfort."

"Should I tell you that she's going to recover?"

"No," she said. "I know better." She shuddered, and he took her in his arms. For the first time, their parting hug was only comfort, not passion. He told her that he planned to drive her to the hospital Sunday morning.

"You can't," she said. "It's hours of travel, longer each way than the time I'm there."

"Which means that I'll have more time with you than your mother will. Why not? Besides, you're running damn-near on empty. If you fall asleep at the wheel and crash your car, both of us will lose you." It was like the kiss down there had been. She could see that it was wrong, but she couldn't resist. Thursday night and Saturday night, their parting kisses were passionate, but their earlier conversations were all about her worries.

Sunday morning, he was outside her door at 6:00. He looked more likely to fall asleep at the wheel than she felt. He drove well, though. It was the first time she had ridden with him in the daytime. She had hardly seen him in the daytime.

"So tell me about your life in Tempe," he said when they were on their way. He had never heard that she waited tables in Tempe. He seemed to assume that college students did no work but studying.

"And what is it like to be an archeologist?" she asked.

"You ever try to put one of those jigsaw puzzles together when a couple of pieces are missing?"

"All the time." She hadn't worked a jigsaw puzzle in years, but when she had they usually had missing pieces. His idea that normal meant always having new puzzles with all their pieces showed her, once more, what a privileged childhood he'd had. New clothes had been a struggle for Mom to buy her. A new toy had been a twice-a-year event.

"Well, archeology is like putting together a puzzle with the great majority of the pieces missing. What they had committed to memory is, of course, gone. The Sumerians were good little boys and wrote on clay. For important stuff, they baked the clay, and we have lots of that. Other cultures used stuff like paper, and that hasn't lasted so well. And, really, when they have writing, that's your field, history. Archeology is about other evidence. But some things last, and other things don't. We have to figure out how people lived by what they left behind."

He went on a little more, but soon they were silent. He woke her when they were close to the hospital.

"You go up," he said. "I've got reading matter."

"Well, I now have your cell number. I'll call you if I need you."

Mom was awake this time.

"How are you feeling?" she asked Mom.

"How do you expect me to be feeling? At least, they give me pain medicine when I need it." She pointed to something attached to her arm. "I knew you were coming, so I stopped pushing it."

"I've been keeping the diner open," she said.

"Good for you. Feed them, and they'll keep you fed, too.... What about your seducer?" Mom never let up on you. Well, she'd got through high school with good grades and no pregnancy, and she was still keeping the diner open. Mom had succeeded by never letting up.

"Greg drove me down here. Would you like to talk to him?"

"Hell no! I talked to him too much. He said that you're going with him might be the biggest mistake you'd ever make. Then he said that your not going with him might be the biggest mistake you'd ever make. He didn't seem to see which. I could see it, easily. Going with him would ruin your life." As though her life wasn't already ruined.

"Well, Mom, you have your opinion, and I respect your opinion. It is, however, my life. And I have to make the decision." They went on for a long time. First, about that, then about what Anne should do about the diner, then about good things from their past. They had some good parts in their past, even if the diner had been open every Christmas and every one of her birthdays. She hadn't even known Mom's birthday until she had to ask as a high-school junior.

Finally, Mom rang for a bed pan and asked her to leave. She went out in the hall and called Greg. He was still in the lobby.

"You didn't have to wait here," she told him when she got there.

"Well, I had reading material, and having brought a friend to visit her mother who was a patient is a perfectly good excuse for being here. Where else in town is it a good excuse?"

"They asked you?"

"Yes," he said. "Security wouldn't be doing its business if they hadn't. On the other hand, when they got my answer, they left me alone. How was she?"

"She doesn't like you."

"Well, the feeling isn't reciprocated. On the other hand, that's like security. I want to take you away from her, so of course she doesn't like me. On the other hand, she raised you, and I like the results, so of course I have to appreciate her."

"How many hands was that?" she asked. He looked thoughtful.

"Only two that time, I think. A raving beauty once said that I talked like a professor. Probably, 'On the other hand' is part of that."

"A raving beauty talked about you?" She wasn't willing to let that compliment go undenied. It was absurd. "I'm jealous."

"The next time you look in a mirror, spit. Are we ready to go?"

"I think so." So they went out into the morning heat. The Jeep was an oven, and he both opened the windows and turned on the air. When the air started blowing cold, he closed the windows.

He got her to the diner in time to prepare for the day. He ate lunch there before driving back.

Greg was closing down the dig. Some things had to be recorded more carefully. He got into every trench and photographed the walls. He supervised the boxing of all artefacts and the labeling of the boxes. The generator was fine for lights; it and the Xerox machine didn't get along. Still, he made several copies of all lists and filed one in his personal papers. If you threatened him, you could get his wallet; he would fight to the death to keep his briefcase.

He drove Anne once more to the hospital and back. He warned her that he wouldn't be available the next Sunday.

"You didn't have to do it at all, ever," she said. "I'm used to taking care of myself."

"Too used."

Friday was his last day. He went to the diner for a late dinner. He swept out one last time, and he kissed her a very long good-night. Then he got into the Jeep and headed out. When he got sleepy, he checked into a motel. He had a hot shower before bed and another in the morning. They were his first since June.

He got to the apartment the next night. The air smelled dead, and he opened the windows. He called Anne at 10:10.

"I miss you," he said.

"It's been one day. You used to wait two days between visits."

"Well, I missed you then, too. But the distance makes it worse."

"Well," she said, "I miss you, too." They talked for a while more, but there wasn't really any news but that.

Anne did miss Greg. Happy as she was that he had called, the voice in her ear wasn't at all as comforting as his arms around her. And when she drove to the hospital Sunday, she found that she missed his company as much as his driving skills. She could handle the trip easily, more easily than the visit, actually. It was just that she felt the concentration she had put in draining her by the end of the day.

One night, he told her that he couldn't call the next night. A formal dinner with presentations was scheduled for that night. She found that she missed the phone chat as much as she had missed the hugs. Still, with the explanation, she knew that he was on her side. He called the next night at 10:10.

Meanwhile Mom was getting worse. The doctor told her that one reason that Mom was allowed to control her own pain medication -- within permissive limits -- was that there was no danger of addiction setting in. He didn't quite say it, but she understood that Mom wouldn't live long enough for that to be a problem. Then her kidneys mostly shut down. The hospital put her on dialysis.

"Your seducer still in town?" Mom asked one Sunday.

"Greg has been back in Colorado teaching college for weeks now?"

"When you go out, tell the nurse to bring me the DNR sheet, will you?"

"What," she asked the nurse at the station, "is DNR." The nurse looked away, and then she looked straight at her.

"Do Not Resuscitate. Your mother had it prepared, then she said she wouldn't sign it until she had talked with you. Really, you know, she's going. Her organs are either going malign or shutting down. We can't keep her alive. Do you want her body to outlive her?"

Anne cried, but the nurse was right. Mom was right. Mom was right about this if not about Greg.

"Mom waited 'til you were out of my life," she told Greg that night.

"Am I out of your life?"

"No, but I didn't tell her that."

"You are one brave woman," he said, "and she's a brave woman, too. It's harder on you. When she goes, you'll still be here to know that she's gone. I wish I could be with you."

"I wish it, too. Oh, how I wish it."

"Well, I need you, but she needs you much more." And the diner needed her, too. She was running the diner mostly for Mom. It still made a profit and fed her, but she had waited tables in Tempe. She didn't need the diner for that. She needed Molly's Diner going on to demonstrate to the town -- maybe to herself -- that Molly was still going on.

Greg talked to Anne almost every night. He knew her schedule, and he called shortly after the diner closed. He tracked her mother's decline partly by Anne's factual reports -- dialysis didn't sound good -- and more closely by Anne's tone of voice.

One Wednesday afternoon, his cell vibrated when he was talking with some students after class. He kept it silent all day. It was Anne's number.

"Pardon me," he said. "I have to take this." He walked away, and the students continued arguing, but without a referee. "Yes, Anne."

"Mom passed this morning."

"Oh, I'm so sorry for you." Anne's mother hadn't only been her only parent, she had been the only relative she knew, nearly the only friend.

"The funeral is Saturday. Can you come?" She asked if he could come. If Anne needed him, he would walk that far.

"Of course. In Randolph?"

"No. The hospital has some arrangement with a funeral home here in Flagstaff. I have the details somewhere, but I can't seem to find them." From the sound of her voice, Anne was so deeply in tears she wouldn't be able to see to read. "I'll e-mail you."

"Of course. Do what you have to do. Depend on others to take care of the other necessities. If something drops off, let it lie." He was giving great advice. Someone else's loss was so easy to figure out.

"Well, Molly's Diner is closed at midday. No lunch, no supper. Even when Mom went into the hospital, I served both lunch and supper."

"Nobody but you puts those demands on you."

"Somebody else did, but she's gone." Then she broke into tears and he tried to make soothing sounds. Suddenly she broke the connection.

That night, though, she sent him an e-mail giving the time of the service and address of the funeral home. He got a flight reservation, a motel reservation, and a car rental over the Internet that night. He didn't want to be without wheels in a strange western city. Anyway, he might need to drive to Randolph. The next day, he visited a local florist's and arranged for a tasteful bouquet via Teleflora.

His cell sounded at 10:30 that night.

"You didn't call," she said.

"I didn't know what you were doing. I'm sorry. Do you need to talk? Does talking do any good?"

"Yes and no. Yes, I need to talk. No, it doesn't do any good."

"Well, I'm here. I'll be in Flagstaff Friday night. You want the name of my motel?"

"Yeah," she said. He gave her all the information. He felt she needed to deal with particulars now. Even if she wouldn't use the details, dealing with details was something that would anchor her. It might have helped; she sounded less frantic.

Friday, after he got his car and got checked in at the motel, he called her again. It was after 11:00, but waking her up was less of a danger than letting her feel alone. It turned out that she wasn't alone. Karen was with her.

At the funeral service, there were two couples and two college-age girls from Randolph, Karen, himself, and -- of course -- Anne and the staff. The guy who gave the sermon knew less about Molly than Greg did. His flowers looked like one of three bouquets that the funeral home hadn't provided by themselves.

He was surprised by Karen. She was short -- five feet tall, if that. She was conventionally cute, rather than pretty. The loveliest woman he knew had spoken of her as the prettier roommate.

After the service, Anne invited everyone to a restaurant for dinner. He was the only man at the table with Karen, Anne, and the two girls that Anne had known in high school. They were Barbara and Honey. They might have been college-age, but it seemed that neither was in college.

When the check came, he covered it with his Master Card immediately. He gestured that the waitress should charge the other table for that, too.

"Greg, you shouldn't," Anne said. She was getting cash out.

"Yes, I should." Somebody should take care of the waif. She was too used to taking the world's burdens upon herself.

He found that Barbara and Honey were riding back to Randolph with one of the couples. Anne and Karen were staying at the same motel he was. He drove Anne back, and she had him stop at a drug store for a minute. She insisted that he shouldn't follow her in. Figuring that it was some feminine product, he waited patiently.

Later, he joined the women in their unit. He learned a good deal more about Karen. She told them a story about why Barbara and Honey chose to ride back with the one couple instead of the other. The story was rather raunchy, but fairly funny. They laughed, and when Anne laughed, she collapsed with laughter. Then she was crying her eyes out. He took her in his arms.

"That's much better," Karen said. "She cried twice in my arms yesterday, but she really wanted yours."

"The bastard didn't now Mom at all," Anne suddenly said. He figured that she meant the presiding clergyman.

"No. Even I could tell that. Do you wish you'd done it in Randolph?"

"No. I don't think either preacher there would have done it." Greg thought she was being too hard on the local clergy, but he didn't know the people.

"I'm sorry I didn't bring flowers," Karen said.

"You brought you," Anne said. "That was what I needed." They spoke a little more about the service. Karen delivered messages from classmates and dorm mates. He got the definite suspicion that Karen had gone around asking, "What shall I tell Anne you said?" Maybe not. Maybe all these people had heard about Anne's mother and did decide to express their feelings to her roommate. Finally, he excused himself.

He was getting ready for bed a quarter of an hour later, when there was a knock on the door. He wasn't expecting anybody, but he pulled on his suit trousers and simply belted them. That was decent enough for a minute's exposure, and he had packed neither pajamas nor robe.

When he opened the door, Anne was standing there.

***

Anne got up and went to the closet when Greg had gone. She took off her dress and hung it carefully in the closet. This was one of the funeral expenses. It was the most expensive piece of clothing that she'd ever purchased. She took off the slip and hung it up, too. The dress required a slip, and her other clothes didn't. She went back to her chair to take off her pantyhose.

"He cares for me," she told Karen.

"Definitely."

"He sent flowers. Mom was mean to him and he sent flowers."

"I'm sorry I didn't," Karen said.

"That's okay. I know how much you stretched to be able to come. But he sent them. Hundreds of people in town ate at the diner and knew Mom. Four of them came for her. Honey and Barbara came for me, just like you and Greg. Those four brought flowers. It's a long way to drive. I know it's a long way. She knew it was a long way, 'cause she used to drive it for radiation. Still, it's not a long way to send flowers. You deal with the florists here."

"Then he comes, all that way," she continued. "I send him an e-mail saying where and when one night, and -- when I call the next night -- he tells me when he'll get here and where he'll be. Then he pays for the meal."

"He had a card. He's one of them." Karen had waited tables. She had only worked summers, but she had enough experience to know about the people who had credit cards and were casual about expenses.

"Well, he left a tip." Some of the people who didn't care what things cost did, some of them left quite generous ones. Some of them didn't care what things cost them, and didn't worry about what things cost their waitress, either. Those didn't bother to leave tips.

"He knew you would notice," Karen said. She couldn't argue with Karen about that. But he had given her a generous tip the first time they had met. Not afterwards -- it would have felt too much like he's paying for the making out -- but the first time.

"Well, he is either sensitive enough to know that I would notice or the kind of guy who always leaves a tip," she continued. "There is no downside to that. And he does like me." She had the rest of her clothes off now, but she had to make Karen see that this was the right thing to do.

"You said that before," Karen said. "I agreed with you then. He likes you a lot."

"And I love him. You say that makes it okay." She went to the closet to put on her dress again.

"Well: Is it okay? Is it okay on the night of your mom's funeral? Those are two different questions."

"Well, it's not like we'd be together tomorrow night. He's leaving. He wrote me that."

"That dress looks wrong." Karen said. "It needs the bra." She took the dress off, and Karen brought the bra over to her. "You really haven't done it with anybody?"

"No, not really, but we got close." She put the bra on, and then the dress again. "How does it look now?"

"Well, okay, for the hundred feet," Karen said. She put her slippers on. They were ratty ones she had bought used in Tempe and worn for another year. "I'm not sure that those do."

Even so, she was going to wear them. Heels wouldn't do. She unpinned her hair, picked up the package from the drugstore, and headed out the door. She was exposed to the whole city as she walked to Greg's door. She took a deep breath before knocking.

Greg gaped at her. She was still wearing the dress that she had worn for the funeral, but she had Bunny slippers on her feet. And her lovely hair was down where it could be seen.

Anne was awfully nervous. She asked, "May I come in?" He stepped aside, and she closed the door behind her. She was still nervous, but nobody from the motel would challenge her now. She didn't know what to do with the package in her hand. She really didn't know what to do about anything. He was supposed to seduce her, but he was only now getting his mouth closed.

Greg couldn't figure what to do with Anne. He wanted to console her; he wanted to sweep her into his arms and kiss her senseless; he wanted to toss her onto his bed and take what she had nearly given him a month before. He was acutely conscious that he had belted on his trousers without closing the zipper. The opening was over on his left leg, but he was getting an erection, and it didn't like the feel of the wool dress trousers against it.

"I'm not properly dressed," he said.

Anne had noticed that. His chest looked nice, paler than his face, but with lots of hair. She could remember how that hair felt. She walked up to him. When he kissed her, she dropped the package from the drugstore on the bureau. She put both hands on his face and made the kiss last. When he licked her lips, she opened her mouth. He teased her tongue with his.

Greg was of two minds -- two bodies, really. The top half was enjoying the taste of Anne's lips. She held his face, and his hands stroked her back. The bottom half included his erection pressing against wool and the slight breeze blowing through his open fly on his left hip. Anne had wanted to come into his room, she had wanted to kiss him. He was open to any idea she had, especially the last, but he did wish that he had enjoyed a one minute warning to get properly dressed. On the other hand, he was drowning in the sweetness of Anne's mouth.

Anne had planned to let Greg take control. He was, however, not going beyond the first kiss, while she had already decided everything. She was ready to be naked under his naked body right now. She felt all the muscles down his back, and he cupped her bottom in his hands and drew her against him. That felt great, but then he let go. She turned her back to him.

"Get the zipper," she said. He did, without much fumbling. He even managed to open the clasp on top she had forgotten to mention.

Greg drew the zipper all the way down. He saw that she wasn't wearing any panties. He let go of the dress. She walked to the closet and took the dress off. When she turned around, the hair on her delta was a darker auburn than the hair on her head. He'd only seen it in the moonlight, and he hadn't seen any color then.

"Anne," he asked, "are you sure?"

Anne walked over to the package from the drug store. She took out the packaged contraceptive and handed it to him.

"Yes, I'm sure." She started to take off her bra. He didn't seem about to, and she remembered the kisses skin to skin. Greg was, at least, getting the box from the store open. She went over to him and undid his belt. His pants dropped, and his penis popped up. It didn't quite look like the illustrations in the sex-ed books, but those pointed either up or down, and this one seemed to be pointing out but rising.

Greg was naked with a naked Anne. He'd spent two months trying to get to that point, but he felt that the night after her mother's funeral was hardly the time. On the other hand, he'd said that she should decide, and she certainly looked like she had decided. He tossed the empty box towards the dresser and stood with the wrapped condom in his hand.

"Shouldn't we go to bed?" he asked. She walked to the bed and sprawled there with her legs spread. Okay, the sight of what she had between her legs was sexy as hell. Still, this wasn't the way he pictured Anne. "Give me a little space," he said. He moved her leg and lay down beside her on his left side. She was in the middle of a twin bed. That didn't leave much room, but it was probably much better than a blanket on the hard ground.

Anne thought she had left him plenty of room with her spread legs. Wasn't that where the man was supposed to go. Still, his kisses were pleasant and his hand stroking over her was sexy. Her nipples hardened in anticipation as his mouth started its leisurely journey down her neck toward them. She felt her folds swell as his fingers twirled the hairs on her delta.

"Have I said your hair is pretty?" he asked.

Greg cupped her mound. His palm was crushing her pubic hair, and his fingers were on the folds between her legs.

"This is lovelier." He kissed her lips again, sparks flew from their tongues as they met. He moved over to her nipple. His finger parted her lower lips as he sucked her nipple.

Anne was feeling feverish. She was aroused and wanting more arousal. She had bravely planned for his possession of her, but it still frightened her. Why couldn't he do it now?

"Let's hurry," she said. Greg's response sounded between a cough and a bark. Did he intend a laugh?

"Indulge me."

Greg was determined that his first full sex with Anne burn every experience she had ever had of other men out of her memory. This might be the wrong time, but it was the right woman, and he was determined to be the right man for her.

"Indulge me," he repeated. He felt her moisture and gloried in it. He got his finger almost where he wanted it. Then he left her nipple and kissed down into her cleavage. He kissed up the further breast. His finger stroked across her nubbin just as his tongue licked that nipple.

She responded! He could feel her stiffen along the entire length of their bodies' contact. He kissed down the bottom side of that sweet breast.

Anne felt hot all over. Yet she shivered. Greg's kisses traveled down across her stomach getting nearer and nearer to the place where his hand was arousing her. Finally, he did take advantage of the space she had cleared for him by spreading her legs. Then his lips were where his hand had been.

As his tongue licked her there, heat spread through her stomach and thighs. She raised her hips off the bed to push herself into his mouth.

Then fire crashed through her. She was burning up, writhing on the bed as on a grill. Even so, it was intense pleasure. It was so much pleasure that she couldn't contain it. She felt it spilling out of her fingers and toes and scalp. She moaned.

Greg stopped his attention to her genitals when he heard that moan. Holding himself up so that he didn't put his weight on her, he kissed up her quivering abdomen. He kissed the smoothness of her breasts with only his mouth and the outside of his knees touching her. He licked one nipple and then the other. He raised himself a little to appreciate her face and the flush that spread from it to her delightful breasts. He kissed the tip of her nose. She seemed to be breathing more easily.

He shifted his weight onto his left arm and reached down to their genitals. He touched his own erection -- his bare erection. The condom was still in his left hand, and he brought his right to meet it. He got the packet open, and then rolled the condom down over himself. Shifting positions again, he opened her lower lips and fit himself between them.

"Say yes, darling," he said. "Oh, Anne please say yes."

Anne said, "Yes!" She wondered for a moment what he thought she had been saying up to then. Then he pressed against her down there.

Greg pushed forward a bit and felt resistance. He adjusted his balance again. Then he thrust. The resistance disappeared, and he felt himself slide in.

Anne had been quite uncomfortable for a second. Then she felt herself being spread, being filled where she was terribly empty and had never realized it. Then she was full and Greg was looking into her face.

Greg was in her all the way, in her warmth, in her slickness. And he was in Anne! He bent and kissed her on the mouth before raising himself and looking at her face from inches away.

"Oh, darling. Oh, Anne. Oh, love. My darling."

Anne had been doubtful of this intercourse business for one moment. It hadn't been all that comfortable to begin with, and when that was over and he was inside, she was carrying rather more weight than she would have chosen, even though it was Greg's weight. What Greg had done with his mouth had been wonderful; this hadn't.

Then he was calling her all those wonderful names. Even his tone when he said "Anne" was delightful. Hearing those was everything the books had promised. She put her arms around that dear -- but rather massive -- body above her and hugged him closer.

Greg took Anne's embrace as acceptance. He moved slowly in and out watching her face for her response. She looked both pleased and loving when he began. As for him, moving through her warm clasp was the finest sensations he had ever received. She started to look worried, and he almost told her that he had remembered the condom. His arousal and the acute sensations from below tangled his tongue. Before he could get his thoughts together, Anne's expression turned inward.

He took that as permission to focus on his own exquisite sensations. He shifted his position to hold a firm breast in each hand. He was gritting his teeth to prevent his going off too soon. She was so lovely, so tight around him.

Then he saw her grimace and felt her clench around him at the same time. He drove into her and pulsed, and pulsed, and pulsed.

Anne felt the fire pour through her again. She was vaguely aware that she was contracting around something, then acutely aware that she was contracting around Greg. He was throbbing, too, in a different rhythm from hers.

Then he was simply a weight on her -- a dear weight, but a suffocating weight, too. When he moved off, she was conscious of him slipping out, much softer than he had been coming in. He pulled her against him. After a minute, though, she realized that she had to go back.

Greg was enjoying the warmth of Anne against his front and trying to ignore the edge of the bed threatening his back. Then Anne was moving. He took up the vacated space, but she was getting up.

"Stay here," he said. "Sleep in my arms." There was a second bed, but that was much too far away.

"I can't. Karen is expecting me."

"Call her. Tell her you're staying."

"I don't have my cell," Anne said.

"Do you know her number?" He got up and gave her his cell. He noticed the condom dangling from him rather obscenely. He went into the bathroom to dispose of it. He washed himself when he was there, and came out ready for bed -- more than ready for a bed with Anne in it.

Anne had Karen's number engraved on her memory. She called her on Greg's cell.

"Hello?" Karen, of course, hadn't recognized the number, an out-of-state number to boot.

"This is Anne. It's Greg's cell if you want to add it to your phone book. He wants me to stay. I'm staying."

"Well, duh!" Karen seemed to think that staying with Greg was more obvious than she did.

"Want the bathroom?" Greg asked. She took the opportunity. Really, a woman with forethought would have brought something. All she had was soap and water. She realized that a woman with more experience would have brought at least a hairbrush and makeup for the next day.

When she went out into the room bare, seeing Greg with his glasses back on and a sheet covering him, she thought of something else she should have brought -- a robe, nightie, or both. The trip to the bed with his eyes devouring her nakedness was miles long.

Greg had first turned on the bedside lamp and turned off the overhead light. Then he had brought up the last number called and entered it in his phone list as "Karen." Then he'd got into bed and awaited his love.

Probably she didn't find his ogling all that loving, but he couldn't resist. At least, when he pulled open the sheet, she hurried into bed. He pulled up the sheet and tucked her in. He kissed her forehead before turning off the lamp. He slipped down into the sheets beside her.

"May I hold you?" he asked.

"Always." She went into his arms, face to face. This was probably not all that useful for sleeping, but the kisses were too delightful to resist. Finally, she saw that the position was impractical. She turned over and backed into the spoon. His nose was buried in her hair, and his hand held her breast. His groin was against her firm, round hips. One part of the groin reacted predictably.

"Do you want to do it again?" she asked.

"'Do I want to?' Indubitably. 'Am I able?' That's much less certain. Luckily, there was only one condom, and that is gone forever. So we aren't going to test my abilities this soon afterwards."

"Doesn't it hurt?"

He laughed. "One of the detriments of coeducation is that it exposes young girls, like you were, to high-school boys. No. It doesn't hurt. It feels delightful in its present location. I like to see your figure, and I like to feel it with my hands, but that's not the only part of me which enjoys the feel."

Anne had not, as a matter of fact, ever been told by a boy that his erection would remain painful until she relieved it. When she thought about what Greg said, she remembered a couple of girls -- Honey who had come to the funeral was one of them -- giggling about boys' lines, including that one.

Her struggles in high school had been over whether she would keep her bra on. Nobody had made a serious effort for her jeans. She had gone to both proms and worn a dress -- the same dress -- to both. Both dates had tried to get their hands under her skirts, and neither had been surprised that he had failed. The more successful Lotharios had taken their steadies to the prom; only the losers had asked Anne.

Even her college romances were limited by the hours she worked. Tom and Barry had each managed to get her jeans off, but not her panties. And then the most romantic visitor in town since the Civil War had wanted her, and taken her to heaven, and said that he loved her. Of course, he had been rather involved at the time. She might not have much experience, but she knew that men would say anything to get into -

- or when they were in -- women's vaginas. Did Greg think she was his love now?

"Was I all right?" she asked. She had felt quite inadequate when she began. After that, she had forgotten her inadequacy because she had been so involved in her own sensations. Not knowing what to do and then forgetting you were supposed to do anything didn't seem like a sound foundation for a good performance.

"Well, does the category 'all right' include 'spectacular,' 'magnificent,' and 'outstanding'?"

"You're sweet."

"You, my darling," he said, "are the sweet one. I suffer from a poor vocabulary. To be fair to myself, though, I don't think the English language contains words to express how wonderful you were."

Greg thought he had gone astray again. He'd talked about how she had been when he should have expressed that she was wonderful right then. She didn't seem displeased, though. She snuggled against him quite arousingly.

They were lying apart when he woke in the morning. He got to the bathroom and emptied his bladder. While he was there, he brushed his teeth and shaved. If he were going to wake sleeping beauty with a kiss, it should be a kiss that didn't make her shudder. If she didn't shudder, she didn't stay after the kiss, either. Anne soon left the bed for the bathroom.

Anne had loved waking to Greg's kiss. The taste of toothpaste in his mouth, however, had suggested that she didn't taste as good as he did. Besides, she needed to use the facilities. When she had flushed and washed her hands, she stuck her head out the door to ask if she could use his toothpaste. Her nakedness bothered her, and she only let her face show.

"Certainly," he said. "The brush, too, if that doesn't gross you out." Her using the brush after he had didn't bother her. Making him use it after she did. She 'brushed' with one finger. Whatever decay germs survived that, the taste wouldn't.

The bathroom was generously supplied with towels. She considered wrapping one around her waist and using another to cover her breasts. That wouldn't leave any bath towels if he wanted a shower, though. She compromised between modesty and practicality by tying one around her neck in back. It covered her in front to mid thigh.

"Come back to bed," he said when she came out. "Please. We have to talk." Well she didn't see anything to talk about. Anyway, they could talk when she was standing up -- sitting down for that matter. He probably wanted to kiss, really. At that thought, she went to the bed. He was lying on the side nearest the bathroom, and she had to walk around the bed to get on her side. To block his view, she partly walked sideways and partly moved the bottom of the towel with her left hand.

She slid beneath the sheet and untied the towel. She tossed it onto the other bed. He took off his glasses and grinned at her. She'd been right; he wanted to kiss. When his tongue touched hers, she started to get warm again. His hand was stroking her back, leaving it warmer. Then he was sucking her tongue, they were lying face-to-face, and they were pressed against each other from lips to her toes.

He was holding her seat to pull her closer, and he felt awfully hard and hot against her stomach. Well, he felt free to put his hands on all of her. She reached between them. When she touched it, he dropped away and onto his back. She pulled her hand back.

"Be my guest," he said. "Explore all you want." So she pulled the sheet back from him and reached out again. It was hotter than the rest of him. It was so soft on the outside, but hard underneath. It was sticking up and curved towards his head. The shaft looked long and thick, and then it got thicker until it narrowed to a point. The head was softer underneath than the shaft had been. He shivered when she touched it.

"Those are very delicate," he said when she moved to the part below, his testicles. They were very hairy, and they didn't look delicate at all.

"Those make the sperm?" she asked. She didn't know why she'd made that a question. She probably knew as much about the theory as he did.

"Yeah." He sounded both tense and pleased.

"Well, you put your hands all over me," she said.

"Let's make that a rule. You can touch me everywhere, and I can touch you everywhere." Somehow, he seemed eager for that statement. She trusted him. After all, she had trusted him with her virginity. And, when he had touched her everywhere, she had enjoyed it immensely. Still, she was suspicious of him right now.

"Only the first part is a rule. I can touch you everywhere, but you can only touch me when I allow you to."

He laughed. "You have me by the balls, and my heart and mind will follow. Look, I'm scheduled on a plane out of Flagstaff at minutes after 11:00. What's your schedule?"

"I have an appointment with Mom's lawyer Monday. I thought I'd go out to see the grave today. I couldn't bear to watch them put her under the ground. Was that weak of me?"

"Sweetheart, you are the strongest woman I know. You have that from her." She loved to have him call her sweetheart.

"That's your rule," she said. "I can touch you any place I want, and you can call me sweetheart any time you want."

He grabbed her then and pulled her into a kiss. Their tongues met, he breasts were pressed against his chest with only two folds of the sheet between and his hands were all over her back. She felt possessed, and very much in love.

"And what do I have to give you so I can call you 'beloved,' or 'darling'?" he asked.

"Another kiss like that." But it wasn't like that; it was even better. He moved the sheets out from between them. He lay flat on his back and lifted her over him. The kiss went on and on. His tongue was everywhere in her mouth and his hands ran up and down her back when not pulling her seat so that she was pressed against him. Her hands hadn't such freedom, but they felt the strong muscles in his arms.

When they finally relaxed, he kissed the side of her neck and her shoulder. She was sprawled face-down over him. She might never have moved, might have missed her lawyer's appointment 48 hours later, if his ring tone hadn't sounded.

"Huh?" he said, "but you're here." He fumbled for the phone on the night stand and found it. "Greg Thibault." Then "Sure. It's for you." he handed her the phone, but held her when she tried to climb off him.

"It's nine-fifteen," Karen said in her ear. "When I called you, this phone rang. How'd you call me last night?"

"I used his. You want to meet for breakfast, I suppose."

"I want to hear all the gory details."

"Well, I don't want to wear the dress again," she said. "How about your bringing my top, jeans, and some underwear over here?"

"Better yet," said Greg, "Why don't I go pick them up in, say, ten minutes?"

"I can hear him," Karen said. "Where is he?"

"Girl, you don't want to know," she said.

"Wanna bet?" asked Karen. "Anyway, I can wait for him to pick up the clothes. Ten minutes, tops."

"She says ten minutes, tops," she told Greg. That got him moving. He lifted her off him and set her to the side of the bed. He got up and rushed to the bathroom. She could hear the shower running when Karen spoke again.

"What was that I heard?"

"Curiosity killed the cat. Anyway, I can't be overheard now."

"You happy?" Karen asked. "You still in love?"

"Very! That answers both questions. If I had it to do over, there are more things I'd bring with me. You couldn't send my brush and my makeup with those clothes, could you? I wouldn't do anything else different."

"I couldn't figure out what you were doing this morning. You only bought one contraceptive, you know. And you always wake up so early."

"That," she said, "is one thing I'd do different. It's something more I'd bring with me, though. And he woke up before I did, too."

"You didn't take any risks, did you? You only bought one."

"We didn't take any risks. It's just that it's so delightful to cuddle."

"Well," Karen said. "I'm happy for you." That was a friend. She heard the shower turn off, and she said goodbye.

"You'll have to use the towel on the bed," Greg said. He was dressing rapidly in khakis and short-sleeved shirt. He sat down to put on his shoes. Watching him dress was fascinating. Besides, she was going to stay under the sheet until he was gone. Then she grabbed the towel and ran to the bathroom.

Greg knocked on Karen's door. Well, it was the room Karen shared with Anne, though not the last night. Karen opened it and let him in. She handed him a bundle of clothes, and then put a brush, some zippered purse-thing, and a cell phone on top.

"You be good to her, see," Karen said. She looked so fierce, although so small.

"I'm going to try."

"She's terribly vulnerable right now."

"I know," he said. "I didn't choose the time. I wasn't trying to get around her when her defenses were down."

"Oh, I know. You'd better take those to her. She'll want the brush first."

So he returned to his room, picturing Anne brushing her hair bare naked. When he got to the room, the shower was running. He checked the bed, and the towel was gone. He set her things down, and started packing. He'd have to be out of here soon.

When the shower stopped, he knocked on the bathroom door. Anne had herself covered with the towel-bib when she opened it. He handed her the brush and then the clothes. She closed the door again, and he wasn't going to get to see her brush her hair after all, even clothed.

She came out dressed in jeans, a blouse, and tennis shoes. She got the zippered container and went back inside. The door was ajar, but he couldn't see in from where he was packing.

Anne puts her makeup on. When she came out, Greg had a suitcase next to the door. When she got her dress and bra, no other clothes were in the closet. She followed him to her room. She hung up the dress again before they all started towards the "lunch room" for breakfast.

Greg said, "Look. I need to check out. Order me waffles and bacon or something. I'll be along." He headed to the registration desk. He checked out and paid with his MasterCard.

"And room 219," he said. "Two girls, Anne Bernard and Karen something. They'll be staying until Tuesday checkout time."

"Check out is at noon, sir."

"I'll pay for them now." The guy raised his eyebrows, and Greg would have loved to wipe that smirk off his face with his fists. This wasn't the time, though, nor the place. The guy did accept the payment.

The girls were eating eggs when he got there, and his waffles were in an unoccupied place. He sat down and dug in. When the waitress brought the check, he used his card again. He folded several singles under his plate, though, when he was done.

"Look," he said, "come to my plane with me. Why not?"

Anne could see many reasons against that. She would have to get back, which would mean that Karen would have to drive her car to the airport, and that would be a traffic snarl in an unfamiliar vehicle. They'd get to the cemetery later than she had planned, and she didn't want to cry when strangers could see. The only reason for the trip was a few minutes more with Greg.

"Sure," she said.

"Wait at the door, dear," he said. "I've got to get my bags."
'Dear'?

"That's another," she told him. "You have to kiss me again to say
'dear.'" So he kissed her right there. The waitress comes to clear their
table had to walk around them. Well, she would find a tip, and the room
was nearly empty. Anne would have walked a few more steps for a tip --
much less a tip that folded -- any day of her working life.

"I do not know either of these people," Karen said to the room at
large. She didn't say it very loud, though. While Greg got his bag, she
gave Karen her car keys. Karen would pick her up at 11:30 at the airport.
She wasn't sure about Greg's flight time, and planes were often late.

Greg's bag was carry-on, and he stood with it and her in the
security line. When the person in front of them was being checked, Greg
pulled a twenty out of his shirt pocket. He pushed it into her hand.

"To pay for the cab," he said.

"But..." she said. Before she could explain that Karen was
coming for her, he was kissing her. He'd started when her mouth was
open, and he thrust his tongue in immediately. He hugged her fiercely,
and she was hugging him back when he tore away. He was taking his
shoes off to be examined, and she would never see him again. She
watched him walk onto the plane while somebody complained about
walking around her. Then she went to wait for Karen.

"Somehow, some tongues in your mouth feel different from
others," she said to Karen as they were driving away. She had never seen
the point of tonsil hockey.

"The woman is in love," said Karen. "Or, at least, in lust. Want to
go to the cemetery now?" So they did. Mom's grave was just a pile of

dirt. She could see the other graves, though, and how hers would look. How long it would be until she could afford a headstone, she didn't know.

She had emptied the cash register, as she did every night. She had emptied the checking account. If the books were accurate, and she was afraid that she didn't keep them as meticulously as Mom had, there would be ten dollars in the account when all the checks cleared. She knew that the diner needed more float than that to operate.

Mr. Munoz, Mom's lawyer, was apparently her lawyer now.

"I'll need one dollar from you to acknowledge that you're my client." She handed it over. "Now, your mother paid me to represent you and give you my best advice. My advice is to walk away from the estate. You're the executor and the beneficiary. You have a certain duty to remain the executor. But the estate is under water. Nobody can make you inherit the debt. Turn the house over to the bank. They'll owe the estate whatever they can sell it for greater than the mortgage amount. I doubt that this will be much. Go to the house today, pack everything which is clearly yours. Put everything that belonged to your mother that you want in a box, several boxes if necessary. Label them 'mementos.' They belong to the estate. Put the diner up for sale. If it brings in more than it owes, the estate is yours. If it brings in less, the estate has negative net worth. Then tell the creditors your buying the mementos for ten dollars. If there is no gold in those mementos, nobody will complain."

"Well, there is her wedding ring."

"Don't leave that in the box. Take it with you. Tell the creditors you're paying twenty dollars for the mementos including her wedding ring. Do you have any idea what it costs to bring a case to court? Sue a daughter for her mother's wedding ring and the judge will be searching precedent back to Spanish and Mexican law to deny you. Not you -- deny them.

"Now, do you have any other way to live?"

"I'm an experienced waitress."

"Well, I hope that you can get work. Your mother had life insurance, but she borrowed against that. She had borrowed almost all the cash value, when she got ill. She tried to keep the premiums up. It would have paid the face amount less the amount of the loan. She was unable to keep up payments, and the last premium was added to her loan amount. That exceeded the cash value and that meant no insurance."

"She used it to pay my tuition."

"Yeah. She was proud of your academic success."

She thanked him, and he repeated his condolences. When she checked out of the motel, she found that Greg had paid for them. Between that and the meals, she had a week's -- two weeks' if she could stretch it -- more living than she had planned for.

She drove to Randolph with Karen. The two of them packed her things in the car and packed a box with her year books and other things she wanted of Mom's. It was a damned empty box. Why, for that matter, did she really want the year books. Mom had prized them, but Anne hadn't looked at them since she got them. The high-school diploma, she figured, she would need.

They had a feast in the diner, two hamburgers apiece. She threw away any food that wouldn't last, even some onions. She got a big piece of paper and wrote "For Sale" on it. She added her cell number and put it in the window. She left Karen in the diner while she drove the garbage to the dump. Then she locked up for the last time.

"I'm going to Phoenix," she said. "No reason for you to take the bus."

"Thanks. If I can cash in the return portion, I'll give it to you."

There was even no reason to go back to Flagstaff. They headed south. Twenty-one years of her life were over, and the remains didn't nearly fill the car.

"I'm so grateful for your support," she said to Karen. "It seemed to me that when all my friends and hers rallied around, only two people showed up." Though six others had attended, and the attorney had been quite helpful. His advice was cold comfort, but she was sure that he had been right.

"Well, if you're grateful, you know what I want now." So Anne told her all that she could remember.

"It hurt?" Karen asked when she got to that part.

"Not really hurt. It was uncomfortable right then."

"Well, rape is often painful."

"Karen!" she said. "Greg didn't rape me."

"I never thought that he had."

"Well, he was willing." Willing? He'd been damned happy. Greg had always been clear about two things. He wanted her, and it was her choice.

"Did you bleed?" Karen asked.

"No. It wasn't like that. You've read too many bodice-rippers." She had always known that Karen read too many of those. She had never known that she believed them.

"When did you tell him that it was your first time?"

"I don't think I did."

"Anne," Karen said. "That matters to guys. You should have told him before you got into bed."

"And I might not have got into bed." That didn't sound right. He hadn't decided that she would get into bed. "Or he might not. You don't know how nervous I was. Every guy who has dated me since high school was an octopus, hands everywhere. Then, the first guy I want, he waits for me to make the advances."

"You sure he's straight?"

"Every time I've been close enough to tell, he's been straight -- and hard. Even right after."

"You," Karen said, "have a dirty mind. My straight-arrow dorm sister."

"Well, I was a virgin then." And Karen laughed with her. She'd been a virgin college girl with a closed mind. Now, she was a woman of the world. They were happy together for an hour more, and she told Karen all about her times with Greg since he walked into the diner. Then, when she mentioned Greg's visiting Mom, her loss caught up with her. She got off onto the side of the road while she could see through her tears. Karen traded seats with her and took the wheel.

She figured that Phoenix offered more opportunities for waitress jobs and lower rents for single rooms than Tempe did. Karen agreed with her. So, she dropped Karen off at the dorm in Tempe and went room hunting in Phoenix. She got a room that night, applied for food stamps the next day, and looked for jobs the next three days. Greg called her Tuesday night.

"Are you keeping going?" he asked.

"Yeah. I closed the diner. I'm looking for work, and I just applied for food stamps."

"Sounds great." Greg clearly had never applied for food stamps in Arizona. It had not been great. "And you're bearing your loss?"

"Yeah. There is something to be said for practical needs. If you don't have food on your table, then you have to put off crying." The comment on food reminded her how much more she had to pay rent and groceries because of what Greg had spent on the motel. "Thanks for paying for my room, by the way, even though I felt sort of. . ."

"That it was a quid pro quo?"

"Something like that."

"Well," he said, "It wasn't. I would have done it, anyway. And you certainly didn't know that I was going to do it."

"Anyway, I'm grateful."

Greg didn't want Anne to be grateful. He wanted her to make her decisions as an independent person choosing her life in terms of her love for him. On the other hand, he didn't want her to starve while she was doing that. He called Karen.

"Hello?"

"This is Greg Thibault, Anne's friend."

Karen figured that she was Anne's friend. Greg was Anne's lover. Still, she couldn't fault him for not using those words to identify himself.

"Yes?"

"I hear that Anne is going through some rough times," Greg said.

"Yes, she is."

"I wish that she would accept help from me," Greg said, "but she wouldn't." Karen wasn't all that sure about that. Anne was a few weeks of joblessness from living on the streets of Phoenix.

"Well," Karen said, "I'd give her any help I could." She was already plotting to smuggle Anne into her dorm room. Unfortunately, she had a roommate. They slept in separate bedrooms, but Deb could never claim ignorance of Anne's presence if Karen got caught.

"And she knows that?" Greg asked.

"Sure." Anne knew she would do anything for her, just as she knew that Anne would walk through fire for her.

"So give me your snail-mail address, your last name for that matter."

Karen couldn't see how giving him her name and address was doing anything for Anne. Still, there wasn't any great revelation. He would know her last name if Anne hadn't been so upset.

"Karen Taylor." She gave him the address.

Greg had been getting in more income than he had been spending every year since he had got his doctorate. He'd put some of that into a money-market account, and let the interest stay there. The morning after his call to Karen, he withdrew three thousand from that account. The deposit in his bank would be by electronic transfer as of the close of business. He wrote two separate checks to Karen for a thousand each. He postdated them a day.

"Sorry for the date on these checks," he wrote. "I'd appreciate it if you'd deposit the second one a week after the date. That would save me a hassle from my bank. If there is a need, however, I'll deal with the hassle. Remember that Anne can't know anything about this. Tell me, preferably before the need becomes acute, if she needs anything else."

Karen hadn't promised Greg to keep anything secret from Anne. Anne kept talking about how bright he was, but he'd heard that Karen couldn't afford to both send flowers and buy a bus ticket. A bright guy should be able to figure out that Anne would know that she didn't have $2,000 sitting around in her bank account. Bright guy? A guy with normal intelligence, a guy who could tie his own shoelaces without assistance, should be able to figure that out.

"I couldn't," Anne said when she saw the letter. "He would think I slept with him for his money."

"Well, first of all, you didn't. I know that; he should be able to tell that. Second, read the letter. He's not doing anything for you. I'm helping out my dorm sister. I am certainly depositing the money in my account." She did, however, honor Greg's request to deposit the second check -- apparently the one with one higher check number -- with a week's delay. With any luck, the first deposit would become checkable before she needed to spend it for Anne.

Anne finally got a job. It was fourteen hours a week, but the guy told her that if she worked out he would give her regular hours. That meant that she would be able to get another job when she knew which hours this place wanted her. They shared tips, which meant that she couldn't use the money immediately. The head waitress, though, had been in her shoes. She told her that she would trust her with a ten buck advance after her second night shift.

Best of all, she worked until after they closed the kitchen. That meant that she could have a meal, and a good meal, after her shift was over. They were expected to wash the dishes, but Anne had washed in a day more dishes than her shift would use in a month.

When her rent came due, instead of promises for later, she gave the guy two weeks rent in a post-dated check from Karen. He bitched, but he knew she had a job, and he knew she hadn't had it long enough to be paid. He took the check. When he got to the point where he could deposit it and it didn't bounce, he was much more polite.

She kept getting calls from Greg, and she tried to keep him up to date on her successes. That she couldn't thank him for his support put rather a crimp in their conversations. Still, they found lots to talk about. "I love you," -- "Oh, I love you, too." She told him her working hours, and he was always careful to call on days she was off.

She got her first paycheck and her first share of the tips at the same time. She went to a bank to open an account with her first check. She realized how much Greg and Karen had helped her. She had been working for more than two weeks, and she had almost no spendable money to show for it. Her share of the tips came to more than a hundred dollars, and that was in cash. She wouldn't be able to write a check for seven more business days. But Karen had given her three checks made out to her landlord and dated on the day that each week's rent was due. The cash would handle food and gas.

The restaurant manager had heard good things about her work. He called her in and offered her a forty-hour week.

"That would be a split shift, though. Breakfast from six to nine Tuesday through Friday. Dinner from five to midnight Thursday through Sunday." Except for Thursday, those were the heavy dinner periods. That meant the tips were heavy then, too. Since they shared them, though, it wouldn't make her tips any larger. Well, since they shared them according to the hours worked, her tips would be something like three times as large.

"It does come," he continued, "with health insurance."

"Why, thank you," she said. "When do I start on the new schedule?" She would start Tuesday. The restaurant was closed on Monday. When Greg called, she told him the good news.

"That's wonderful!" he said. "Does that mean that I should keep my calls to lunchtime since you won't be eating then? Or does it mean I should avoid noon calls because that's the only time you'll have for sleep?"

"Why don't I call you?" She paid her phone bill by check, and it wouldn't be due until her paychecks were good. She'd already paid the last month with a check from Karen.

"Okay. I'll send you my schedule. I don't answer the phone during class, even if it's from you. I can't figure out how to get a special ring tone when everything else is silenced."

"Send me the schedule," she said. "If you said you'd answer when you were in class, I would worry every time I called you that you were in front of a class or something. I don't want you to treat my phone calls as emergencies. I want you to think of them as pleasant chats."

Greg had come to think of them as something between a necessity of life and phone sex. While she never so much as referred to their one night of passion, never even mentioned their times watching the stars, though that could be expressed innocently, he found her recitals of job experiences more arousing than another woman's most explicit description of sexual encounters. When her reports had been of applying again and again without success, his response had worried him. Was it a sign of sadism that he would find Anne's suffering sexually exciting. Now that it was reported of successes, his enjoyment was unalloyed. He didn't mind being sexually aroused by Anne's triumphs.

And he was quite clear that they were triumphs. Anne's family hasn't been able to pay her tuition every year, like his had. She hadn't inherited stock when her parent died. She had been dealt a hard-scrabble hand, and she had won despite that. That she had won games that he had never had to play made her victory more significant, not less significant, than his academic successes.

Anne, both shy and a little peeved, had never mentioned to Greg any help from Karen. She didn't want to think of herself as a kept woman. She certainly didn't want Greg to think of her that way. As long as she was expressing her love for him several nights a week, she was trying to not think about how he'd supported her. She certainly didn't want him to think about it during their talks. Then, too, he had gone to Karen. It was wrong of him not to have approached her directly. That she would have rejected direct help from him was beside the point. If they were going to be in love, they should be totally open to each other.

Greg was perfectly happy that he'd provided money that Anne hadn't needed. She had got a job on time. Well, he had purchased insurance. If he had purchased health insurance for Anne and she had never gotten sick, he would not have complained. Karen was so close to Anne that she would hear about any troubles. She would act to avert them if she had the means. She now had the means. He was much happier that Anne had succeeded on her own.

Now, though, she was employed full time in Phoenix. If he wanted to see her, he would have to go to Phoenix. Unfortunately, he was currently teaching a Saturday morning class and a very-early Monday morning class. That made for a damned-short weekend, especially if two flights had to be fit in as well.

Thanksgiving break was coming up, though. He went to his computer and got himself scheduled flying to Phoenix Wednesday night and back Sunday night. Then he called Karen again.

"Look," he asked, "she sounds okay to me. Do you think the first shock of her mother's death has worn off sufficiently for her to make long-term decisions?"

Karen couldn't figure this guy out. Anne had been making long term decisions since the Monday after the funeral. She had totally changed her life. She had walked away from the house where she had spent 21 years and the business which had been her only other inheritance from her mom. She had got herself a job, and she had got herself a place to stay. Now, a month later, Greg asked if she could make long-term decisions.

Then she relented a bit. If Greg didn't appreciate how thoroughly Anne had coped with her life, he had given concrete help. And, really, despite how great a person Anne was, she had needed that help. Karen thought both of these people were silly in their worries about the appearances regarding that help. She was on the outside, after all, and that's where you saw appearances. They both looked like innocents to her. Still, unworldly as he was, Greg had been a help.

"Sure," she said. "Now, total recovery will take some time..."

"If ever," he said, "I lost my parents years ago -- and it was sudden, not the slow-motion descent into hell that Anne underwent. I don't think I'm recovered yet. Still, there are degrees."

Karen didn't believe she had ever before heard the past for "undergo." Anne had told her about his handing her faculty ID to prove he was a professor. She'd have taken oath on a stack of bibles on the basis of this conversation alone. She had taken Journalism because Creative Writing didn't prepare you for anything; still she thought Anne's guy would make a great character for a short story if anyone would believe him. But she had better say something.

"Yeah. There are degrees, and Anne's past any point where I would worry about her ability to decide."

"Thanks," he said, "thanks a lot. Have a happy Thanksgiving." Which was, in mid-November, a weird good bye. The decorations were up. Hell, some stores had Christmas decorations up. But real people wouldn't think about Thanksgiving for another week.

Greg was, on the other hand, thinking about Thanksgiving quite hard. He made another withdrawal from his money-market account, many times as much money as before. He thought that his trip might prove to be very expensive. His call to Anne was Monday evening. He knew she was off Mondays, and he knew it was too early for her to be asleep. As a matter of fact, Anne was finishing off a supper she had cooked on her hot plate.

"Darling," he began, "can you talk?"

She swallowed. "Sure."

"What would you think of my coming to Phoenix over the Thanksgiving weekend?"

"I would love it."

"Is your landlord a puritan?"

"Well, he's awfully nosy, and the lease says single-occupancy."

"Okay," he said. "Why don't I register at the hotel as Mr. and Mrs. Greg Thibault?"

"I'd love it."

Greg made his reservation, specifying a double bed. He made his purchase. He spent a lot of time dealing with the administration -- especially the admissions office. Time passed. He walked out of his last class before Thanksgiving. He picked up his luggage from his office, and he drove to the airport. He had to change in Denver, but he got to Phoenix before ten and to the hotel before eleven. He rang her.

"I'm here," he said.

"Shall I come over?"

"I don't think so. You have an early morning tomorrow."

Anne was disappointed. She would have loved to come to him whatever the time. Still she was overjoyed when she saw him come into the restaurant at 8:15 the next morning. The breakfast crowd was thinning out, and she had several tables free. She stood by one of them, and he came over.

"What's good?" he asked.

"The western omelette."

"That's it then." She brought him a western omelette and coffee. She felt his eyes on her through the rest of the time. A few minutes before nine, he got up and slipped a bill under his plate. She cleared, and saw that it was a twenty.

"I should have told you," she said when she joined him at the door carrying the plastic bag. "We split tips." Then she had to explain what that was.

"Well," he said, "at least that should make you popular." He had rented another car, and he opened the door for her. "Would you be more comfortable in this coat?" he asked. It was a raincoat and not a cloud in the sky, but she was wearing her waitress uniform. The hotel staff wouldn't believe 'Mrs. Thibault' in a waitress uniform.

She had practiced with Mom's ring. It went over her knuckle with a little Vaseline and a lot of effort. She had the Vaseline on the ring already, and she exerted the effort while he drove them to his hotel.

Nobody questioned them. He led her to the elevator and to his room. He put out the 'Do not disturb' sign and closed the door. They kissed, it was heavenly, but she was soon hot. He took her coat and kissed her again. He took off her blouse and kissed her again. He was reaching for her skirt when she stopped him.

"You have to, too."

"Well, okay." He took off his shirt, and they kissed. They went on like that. When he bared something to her, he kissed that. So she started kissing his body, too. She hadn't known that male nipples responded.

Greg lay his love down on the double bed. He kissed her deeply. Then he kissed down her body. Her breasts were a place of wonder. Her abdomen quivered under his mouth. When he kissed her thighs, she wriggled on the mattress. When he reached her center, her moisture welcomed him.

Anne had been thinking about Greg since she woke up. She had been imagining his penetrating her, possessing her, since she got in the car. She had melted into his kisses. Now, as he kissed her body, she was only conscious of his mouth on her. By the time his kisses reached her mound, she was feeling hot. He licked her. She felt his tongue on her clitoris, and sparks flew inside her.

Greg kept most of his attention on what his mouth was doing, but he used his right hand to raise her leg, then he slipped that arm under it. He did the same with his left hand. When he got both hands on her breasts, he rubbed his thumbs across her nipples. He kept them there while he returned his attention to his mouth. He licked her labia and continued on to her clitoris. She gasped, and he continued to incite her in any way he could.

Anne felt heat pour out of her breasts and belly into the rest of her body. Then fire crashed through her. She writhed as though she was on the grill. She tossed and turned, but still fire poured out of Greg's mouth.

Greg sucked Anne's clitoris until she collapsed. This time, there was a soft and a wide bed for them to share. He moved up that bed to lie beside her.

"Darling, sweet, beloved," he cooed. "You are so wonderful, so sensuous, so beautiful. I love you, and I want you. Right now and forever."

"Love you, too."

Taking that for a sign of recovery, he reached for the packet on the night stand. When he was sheathed, he began kissing her again. Since she was breathing hard through her mouth, he kissed her elsewhere. First, he kissed her face, then her neck, then her breasts. He climbed between her legs, but buried his face in her cleavage and kissed her breast bone. When he kissed up the side of one breast towards the nipple, Anne reached for him.

Anne would normally have regarded Greg's kisses as delightful. She was again feeling empty, though, where she had only been filled once. She spread her legs and reached up with her arms.

"Now?" he asked.

"Now." And it was more now than any other now had ever been. He spread her lips with his fingers and then with his penis. He went into her and went further in. Then he was filling her. He kissed the tip of her nose while he was fully in, then backed out a little and kissed her mouth. The taste wasn't all that pleasant, but that only meant that he had accepted much more of that taste to give her pleasure. She hugged him with her arms and raised her knees to hug him there, too.

"Oh, Anne," he said. He pushed into her a little deeper. Then he was moving in and out. He was on top of her and his hairy chest was tickling her nipples. She could see his face, and he was gazing at her lovingly. She could feel him move within her, slowly, firmly, possessively. Heat spread through her.

Suddenly, flame leaped in her. She writhed to escape the flame -- or, maybe, to get more of it. She felt herself contract and knew she was contracting on Greg. She was filled with such pleasure that she couldn't contain it.

Greg felt her clasp his length. He drove forward though he was as deep within her as he could go. He erupted in her depths. "Oh, Anne," he cried, "oh God!"

When he next could understand his position, he was lying on her softness except where his elbows dug into the mattress. He felt himself slip out of her, and reached down to check that the condom was still on. He moved off her gingerly. He lay beside her.

"Anne," he said finally.

"Greg. I love you, Greg."

"And I love you. I have something to talk about concerning that."

"Great. But wait until I come back." She disappeared into the bathroom, taking the package she had brought from the restaurant. At first, he thought she was answering a call of nature. Restaurants must be harsh environments that way. Then he heard the shower running. Well, that implied there would be no more sex today. Still, he got another packet out of his box of Trojans and tossed the one he was still -- barely -- wearing in the waste basket.

He had a package of his own to present. He got it out of his pants pocket and put it on the night stand. He smiled sardonically when he put it on top of the Trojan packet.

Anne had a brief shower. She dried herself carefully before taking out the nightie she had purchased for this extended weekend. She put it on and adjusted it. She tied the ribbon in front where it closed the nightie over her breasts. Then she reached up to her hair. Knowing how Greg liked it, she unpinned it all and brushed it out. Putting the brush in the bag, she left the room.

Greg reached for his glasses when he heard the door open. As putting them on needed a few seconds and all his attention, he looked up to see Anne in all her glory. Her hair was down and floating freely over her shoulders. She was wearing something blue, which tinged her skin without quite hiding it. Her breasts pressed the blueness out, and he could see her nipples trying to escape that covering. The blue color extended down over the top of her legs, but only the very tops.

Its two sides were held together only between her breasts. That meant that her mound was sometimes covered with two layers which was almost adequate concealment. Sometimes, as she walked, it was covered by one layer, which barely impeded the sight. And, sometimes, both sides flapped free to reveal the auburn adornment that nature had provided to conceal her secrets.

Greg had his mouth open. It was drooling. About half an hour after his previous emission, he was beginning to harden again. When Anne had covered half the distance between them, he remembered to breathe.

Anne was not a cruel woman, and she truly loved Greg. She had always felt like his student, though. He was a professor, and he was her mentor in sexuality. Seeing him stunned gave her a great deal of satisfaction. She was getting her own back.

"Good God," he said.

"You like?" The question was rhetorical. Greg finally remembered to close his mouth.

"You brought that here in that little bag?" She nodded. "Carrying a concealed weapon."

She smiled. "We're very permissive about that in Arizona."

Greg thought that the smile was definitely overkill. She had already rendered him defenseless, and then she brought out a smile that was like an H-bomb. The only reason he hadn't rolled over on his back and played dead for her was that he was too deranged to think how.

Finally, she got into bed and covered it all up except that the shape of her breasts, even the shape of her mound, were molded by the sheet. She looked at him fondly. Less like a woman in love than like the owner of a well-liked -- but somewhat stupid -- puppy that kept stepping on its own ears. Okay, just as long as he was well liked.

"You wanted to talk about something?" she said. Yeah, he had wanted to talk about something. Before the bulldozer had run over him, he had wanted to talk about marriage. At least, he no longer had to worry that his keen intellect was taking advantage of her grief-ravaged state. She was one hell of a lot more compos-mentis than he was right now.

"Yeah. You know, did you enjoy playing the part of Mrs. Thibault right now?"

"I kept being afraid that they would catch me out."

"Well, if you couldn't be caught out? Oh, hell! If I'm not being coherent, it's your fault." He reached for the box and handed it to her. "Anne, would you marry me?" At this point, he didn't even trust himself to open the box.

He hadn't wanted to over-awe her when she was deep in grief and had no place to go. He hadn't wanted to con her into it with his help and her helplessness, because, really, she wasn't helpless at all and she would realize that at some time. He had wanted to make a coherent presentation. Well, that was water under the bridge.

Anne opened the box. The shape was immediately suggestive, and she had heard him say the word "marry." Still the ring was a shock.

"Oh, Greg," she said. She threw her arms around him and kissed him. Because of the way he was sitting on the bed, that meant kissing his ear.

"Is that a yes?"

"This is a yes." she tossed off the covers and tugged the end of the blue bow that was specifically designed for him to tug. As the nightie flew open, she wrapped him in her arms and pulled him down on top of her. She spread her legs to bring him in.

Greg was acting on autopilot now, but his autopilot was programmed for condoms. He reached to the side of the night stand and got it in his first grab. He opened the packet while he was climbing between Anne's legs. When it was on, he positioned himself. At his first touch to her center, Anne grew still. He adjusted slightly to where the opening was. Then he slid deep into her.

"Yes," she said and raised her knees around him.

"Will you?" He pulled out to her entrance

"Yes."

"Marry me?" He drove into her again.

"Yes."

And it went on, question and answer, penetration and withdrawal, love and desire. Her final "yes" was nearly a shout. She clamped upon him rhythmically. He drove all the way into her, and stayed there. Her climax was intensely arousing, but it didn't take him over.

He moved in slow stages while she relaxed beneath him. First, he got on his right elbow, then on his left. He pressed her legs wider with his own legs and then moved his closer together again. When she stirred under him and looked at him, he moved out and then in again very slowly and gently.

"I love you, Anne," he said before moving again. Then the words came along with the strokes. As he sped up, "Love you," became his words on every in stroke.

At his greatest speed, that finally became too much to say. "Love" was drawn out on relatively slow out strokes, then an explosive "You" as he thrust in quickly.

Anne was aroused by both his words and his actions. She had been heated by her previous climax and enthralled by his proposal. His actions felt like he was pumping more love, more arousal, more heat into her with every word and every stroke.

When the flame burst within her, it seemed inevitable. She shook, but her love was shaking her and Greg was shaking her.

Greg felt her contract around him. This time, it did take him over. He withdrew through her clasping walls. Then he thrust inward and pumped himself into her.

When, long afterward, he withdrew, he discovered that it hadn't gone into her after all. They lay side by side and dozed. Whenever he woke it was to remember that he loved her.

When they finally woke together, it was nearly three. After brief showers, she donned her uniform again. He found the ring still in the box on the floor. She got her mother's ring off with a struggle. The new one was too large. He drove her to her rented room. She packed a suitcase with enough clothes for the next three days, and he put it in the car. She found a Band Aid, and put it on her finger so that the ring wouldn't fall off. They ate just before she had to go to work.

He dozed again, but he set his alarm for plenty of time. He got to the restaurant at 11:30. At midnight, when the last few customers were chased out, she brought two servings of one of the meals that hadn't sold so well that night. They ate across from each other. He paid for his meal by card, since he wanted a record that he had. He gave her two dollars to put in the shared-tip jar. They got more suspicious glances from the hotel staff at nearly one than they had in the midmorning. In their room, he persuaded her to sleep without the nightie.

Anne had found that the nightie tended to get all messed up in bed. Greg's idea of their both sleeping nude was more comfortable. Rather than the nightie, she wore him. She kept her robe beside the bed, however. When the alarm went off, she rose, showered, and dressed. Greg drove her to work without even shaving.

He came in for breakfast shaven, however, at the end of her shift. She went home for different clothes, and entered the hotel with Greg carrying the uniform in a bag. Upstairs, they went to bed again.

Greg thought it was a mistake to marry a woman you hadn't kissed. Now, he'd kissed Anne's lips, and the rest of her face, and her breasts -- although maybe not sufficiently. He'd kissed her center, and Anne thought he'd done that very well. There was so much else of Anne that he hadn't kissed, though. He wasn't just going to marry her front. Despite having declared that his idea was silly, Anne didn't seem especially opposed to having her back kissed.

After a bit of this, however, such a brief time that he'd only covered one shoulder blade, she insisted on rolling over and having her mouth kissed again. One thing led to another.

After the intensity, he'd almost say the violence, of the previous day, it was nice to join together and roll onto their sides. He would kiss her forehead; she would kiss his neck; he would pull her closer to him by her rump, and he would go in a little deeper. They would kiss again; he would thrust again.

Anne was enjoying the closeness. She had enjoyed the wildness and the words of the previous day more, but this was something to savor. She supposed that this quietness was what marriage was really about. She was warm all over, and she was growing warmer. She loved Greg, and she loved lying so close to him, kissing him, being kissed by him. Clearly, the fireworks of the previous day were something rare. And, today, she had Greg up against her, and she had Greg inside her. She was content and would be content to go on like this for hours.

Then, totally surprising her, the fire shot through her. She convulsed, and Greg turned her over and fed the fire within her.

Greg was enjoying himself, enjoying the closeness, enjoying Anne's clear enjoyment. Then Anne clasped around him. He went back on top of her, drove in and out through that clasping, and erupted.

When he fell back, he fell apart from her and came out. They were on their sides facing each other again. When his strength recovered, he got the sheet and light blanket and covered them both.

"Dearest," he said. He didn't say or do anything more until Anne got her robe and headed to the bathroom. Then he got up himself and removed a large packet of paper from his suitcase. It was in a manila envelope, and he slipped this under his pillow.

"Come back to bed," he said when she returned. Anne slipped out of the robe and between the sheets without being exposed to the air for more than one second. He got a glimpse of her during that second, though. She lay facing away and moved her sweet, round butt against his middle. "Modesty," he said sententiously, "is inappropriate between a married couple."

"Well," she said, "we aren't married yet." He smiled. He expected the marriage sooner than the end of her modesty. It was too soon to discuss timelines, though. He had another issue that would influence that.

"Is your long-term goal still to be a history teacher?" he asked.

"Well, I'm not sure that it's still possible. It's my dream, though."

"Darling!" The poor girl dreamed of being a high-school teacher. Dreams were for winning Olympic gold or a Nobel prize. Dreams weren't for anything so pedestrian as teaching school. He hadn't dreamed of being an archeologist. Of solving the question of where the Maya went, perhaps, back when he was young and hadn't figured out that the Maya stayed right there. Their high culture evaporated, but the people were still in Yucatan. But you don't dream of being a high-school or even a graduate-school teacher.

"Well, now that you have decided your future marriage status, the next thing to do is to decide your student status," he said. "If we're married, we'll live in the same place. I have a job at the University of Colorado in Boulder. I don't spend all my summers there, but I'm there during the school year. You've seen how short this vacation is. I'd like us to live there."

"Of course."

"Among the compensation that an assistant professor at the University receives is the right to a discount on tuition." He was going to continue, but she interrupted by turning and facing him.

"You mean I could go to college there?" She sounded excited. He'd prepared his arguments for doing that, and she had short-circuited all of them by being excited at the prospect.

"Yeah." He brought out the packet from the university and showed it to her. She got the idea and turned back around to open it. That put her rump an inch or two from his groin. He moved his right leg up the bed to press in the crack between her buttocks.

"To teach in Colorado," he continued, "you would probably have to take some courses you wouldn't need to teach in Arizona. Colorado History is one. At the same time, taking senior courses in the opposite semesters would often be impossible. These two problems would yield to one solution. I suggest you take courses next semester and all the next academic year."

"I could?"

"You'd have to move quickly. They tell me that decisions on admission are separate from decisions on granting faculty-dependants a discount. That is fortunate for us, because you are not a faculty dependant quite yet. For the first semester, you wouldn't be matriculated. That means that they wouldn't actually take responsibility for having admitted you, but they would let you take courses. Then, next fall, in nine or ten months, you would be a fully-admitted student. That would get you out a year later than you had intended when you entered college. On the other hand, you'll get out with more courses -- more information when those are real courses."

Anne was trying to make sense of the tremendous diversity of material that Greg had brought her. She was also trying to listen to what Greg was saying. The written stuff would be here later. Spoken words, when you didn't have a recorder, might never come again. Then she realized that they could come again. This was Greg. They were engaged. She could ask him to repeat anything. She turned to face him again.

"I love you," she said. She kissed him. "Now slow down. I can go back to school at your school? I can live with you and go to school?" That seemed to be impossible. You had to choose which good thing you wanted. Sometimes, like when she had found that Mom was sick, you had to choose which bad thing you could try to avoid.

"You could live with me and go to school. It would really be better for us to be married -- better for me and we get the tuition discount."

Greg wondered where his determination had gone that she not marry him because of the advantages it would bring. Well, she had said that she would marry him.

Anne hadn't considered 'living with Greg' as a contrast to 'marrying Greg.' "That's what I meant. We'd be married, and we'd be living together, and I'd be going to college? Both, I mean all three."

"Yeah. You want to take courses?"

"Oh, yes!"

"Well, it's a shame you won't be taking my courses. I'll be giving other professors what we value most, a student who wants to learn what we teach. Anyway, basically, next academic year you should be taking what the standard senior year for the degrees you want. This next semester is for adjustment. You take whatever Colorado would have given you in your first three years that Arizona State didn't."

"Do you think they teach more?" Anne asked.

Greg really did, but he punted. "Well, they teach different things. Since you want a Colorado degree, you want all that Colorado requires. Where Arizona State requires more, then that doesn't get you any closer to a Colorado degree. For example, you've taken Arizona History; you haven't taken Colorado History. After graduation, of course, those extra courses give you an edge." Greg wasn't certain that Arizona History would give you an edge in getting a teaching job in Colorado. Well, it was another History course. "One thing to watch out for is that when you pass a course with a D, then it gives you credit where they teach the course but it doesn't transfer."

"I didn't."

"No D? How did you do?"

"I can't really remember them all," Anne said. "I got a C four times, and I got a B more often than an A."

He had been worrying about their accepting her. Now he stopped. Most transfer students had been in trouble in their previous school. Anne, who had, of course, had serious personal troubles, had neither academic nor school-behavioral trouble on her record.

"And, when you're sure that you have patched any holes, then you can take any other course for which you have the prerequisites, if that interests you."

"Yeah," she said. "I haven't looked, but the Arizona State catalog was always filled with courses that looked intriguing."

"Have I mentioned that I love you?" he asked. It was really a shame that being his wife was going to preclude her being his student. People who find course descriptions in the catalogs intriguing are a tiny minority, but they are worth their weight in platinum. Professors are people who spend their lives explaining facts they find fascinating to people who are bored with them.

"Not often enough."

"Well, I would get hoarse. I love you. I adore you. You are an absolute delight."

Anne was very careful to put the school packet on the floor by the bed before things got serious.

She dozed off in his arms and snuggled against him when she woke up. She remembered the packet about going to college, but that raised another question.

"Are you awake?" she asked.

"I don't think so. I'm having the finest dream possible. I have my love in my arms, and we're engaged."

"Well, since you're awake, do you know about restaurants in Boulder? I might be able to find another job, but being a waitress is what I know best."

Greg was shocked. If she wanted to teach after she graduated, that was fine; that was a career. Waiting tables was not worthy of her, and they didn't need the money. They could, if it came to that, live together in his apartment, and her merely cooking for him would save more than the cost of her food. He had unspent income, too.

He thought before speaking, though. Anne was a woman who had waited tables since she was old enough for a work permit. Her mother had operated a diner for decades before that. He wasn't going to tell her that her life had been insignificant until he came along. He damned-well wasn't going to tell her that Molly's life had been insignificant.

"Well, dear," he said. "The first semester is going to be full of surprises, and the grades then will be critical for the school's decision about admitting you. Then, too, it's going to be the beginning of our married life, and that will put strains on you, too. Why don't you concentrate on those things? The summer or fall will be soon enough to look for work."

And, of course, when that time came, she would have the experience of college without a job to compete with studying. He could point out the advantages she had experienced.

"Okay," Anne said. She had already found the mere forty hours of her present job a real treat. She got as much sleep as she wanted. That wasn't much when Greg was there, of course, but she had really slept a lot in the first weeks.

That night, she left early. He drove her to her room, and she changed there. They had a meal before he took her to the restaurant. Again, he came in late and they shared a late supper.

"It's not fair," she told him, "that you have to pay for food that they would throw out otherwise."

"Well," he said, "if any one person who ate here didn't have his meal, they would throw it out. If nobody had meals here, they wouldn't cook it. Then they wouldn't pay waitresses."

"Did anybody tell you that you sound like a professor?"

"I can remember a raving beauty saying that. Anyway, I was talking economics, and I don't sound like an economics professor. I can remember my course in Introductory Economics, and it was all about marginal costs being higher than average costs."

"I didn't take that course," Anne said.

"Consider yourself blessed. The restaurant charges for a meal the marginal cost, the cost of feeding the last person who comes in or the additional person who could come in. It's cost per meal, and this is true, is the average of the cost of everything, food, rent, you, over the number of customers. Their profit is the difference -- the marginal cost minus the average cost."

"Well, if another customer comes in, it doesn't cost the restaurant anything. I might work harder, but they don't pay me more -- my share of the tip he leaves is all."

"Yeah," Greg said, "but this restaurant puts the prices on the menus. Economists eat in restaurants which auction off their food."

"Greg, you know one hell of a lot more than I do, but not about restaurants. I think you're crazy."

"Join the club."

She felt sudden remorse. "Crazy, but sweet." He hadn't been trying to persuade her; he had been joking.

"Well, that club has fewer members."

"It has, at least, one." And he was sweet. All her fellow waitresses had already admired her ring. They were all secretly watching them while eating the leftovers, and when the time came to wash up the dishes, Greg joined in. The others all thought that he was a great catch.

He drove her to her room. She changed there. She wasn't going to wear the uniform in the hotel anymore. It was well after one when they got back to their room. Greg hugged her while he was going to sleep, but he didn't go any farther.

When she woke up, the alarm wasn't ringing. The light through the window, though, showed that it was after six. She was up, in the bathroom, and in a dither before she remembered that it was Saturday. There was no work until evening.

It was Saturday, she was engaged, and Greg was in the bed. Life couldn't be better. Greg was starting to wake up when she got back, and she told him.

"It's Saturday, and we're together. What could be better?"

"Hold that thought," he said, "I'll be back in a minute." He disappeared into the bathroom. When he came back -- after a lot more than a minute -- he smelled of aftershave. "It's Saturday morning," he said. "Are you thinking of breakfast or something else?"

"Something else. But how about you?"

"I think I'll have my breakfast in bed." He didn't really begin to eat her, though. A few nibbles with his lips soon turned into kisses.

She was already very warm when he returned to her mouth to give her a deep kiss. His hand, which had been stroking her center, moved more slowly and less firmly. She felt herself rising to meet it more firmly. Then fire swept through her, and she moaned into his mouth.

He moved off her face, but not far. He stopped stroking, and cupped her center. He kissed her forehead, the tip of her nose, her forehead again.

"Dearest Anne, you are so remarkable, so wonderful." He lay down beside her and hugged her with one arm. She waited for more, but he didn't take any action.

"Aren't you going to?" she asked.

"Going to have breakfast? I believe I am. Do you want to eat downstairs, somewhere else in town, or have room service?"

"Let's eat downstairs." Room service sounded awfully expensive, and they would have to get dressed anyway. So they both got dressed and went downstairs.

"Well," Greg said when they had ordered, "I see us as having two tasks today. Aside from the task already completed, of course."

"Well, if you find that task so unpleasant..."

"I didn't say unpleasant. The first is to get that ring of yours shrunk."

"They can do that?" Anne asked.

"They can do that. The jeweler in Boulder would do it, or enlarge it, for free. We can't expect a guy who didn't sell it to do it for free. The second task is to set the time and place for the wedding. That's basically up to you. It needs to be before, preferably well before, the term begins in Boulder." As far as Greg was concerned, the only reason for the delay was the marriage license. Women had other ideas, though, and he wanted Anne to be quite satisfied with her wedding.

"Tempe would all right?" Anne asked. That surprised him. He had expected the site to be Phoenix, where she lived now, or Randolph, where she had grown up. But Tempe contained all the people who had signed the card for her mother's funeral, and Randolph only contained six people who had attended.

"If that's what you want. The location only has to satisfy you. If you'd always dreamed of a wedding in Ulan Bator, I might raise some objections."

"It's more likely," she said, "that you would want the wedding in Ulan Bator, and I would object."

"We're narrowing it down fast. We both agree not to have it in Ulan Bator." She laughed at his silliness.

"Tempe. I should call Karen."

Anne did. When Karen answered, she plunged right in.

"Guess what. I'm engaged."

"To Greg?"

"Well, duh! It gets better. I'm going back to school. His school in Boulder, Colorado. I'm going to be a senior next school year, but I'm going to take some courses next semester. And I'm not going to wait tables that semester."

"You're going to wait tables after that?" Karen asked.

"Of course, but not full time. Want to talk to Greg?"

"Sure."

Greg took the phone. "Greg Thibault here."

"One," Karen said, "congratulations."

"Thank you. I feel like the luckiest man alive."

"Two," Karen said, "it's about time. When is the wedding? Is that going to be another interminable delay because you two are so squishy?"

"You'd have to ask Anne that. I just asked her, myself. It has to be before the start of the next school term, and there is a waiting period locked into wedding licenses. In between that, it's Anne's decision."

"And three, why is she going to be waiting tables? Doesn't a college professor make enough to support a wife?"

"Look," Greg said, "I'll talk to you about that later."

"Yes," Karen said, "you will. Let me talk to Anne again."

Anne took her cell when Greg handed it to her.

"So," she asked, "want to be a bridesmaid?"

"You couldn't stop me. When is it?"

"I don't know. Would the girls stay over another day of Christmas break?"

"To see you married?" Karen asked. "Sure."

"First day of Christmas break work?" Anne asked Greg.

"Yeah. I'd have to have a specific date."

"Karen will know." She turned her attention to the cell.

Greg had planned to get the ring down-sized first and then have a long discussion on time and place. Well, Karen was in the loop on wedding planning, and that was good. He'd ask her later whether she would need more money. He wanted Anne to have the wedding of her dreams. They were in love -- both in love -- but he didn't expect Anne's state to last forever. As far as he could see, his parents, while they had loved one another, had not been 'in love' any time that he could remember. He had seen early photographs, and they had been starry-eyed in them. They didn't look like that in later snapshots. Nor had they looked like that at any time in his memory.

Fine. But when he had more waistline and less hair, he wanted his wife to remember the good times he had given her. That should include the wedding of her dreams. That meant that she shouldn't scrimp, and Karen could persuade her not to scrimp. He would give her a context.

"Look," he said when they were in the car on their way to the jewelers, "I have three confessions to make before we're married. I don't want to marry you under false pretenses."

"I notice you didn't tell me until I'd said yes."

"Well, first thing, you keep calling me a professor. My students do the same, but I'm really an assistant professor."

"I think you told me that," she said. "I've been to school. I don't think there are many full professors as young as you."

"The second thing is that 'Greg' is a nickname."

"That's obvious. For 'Gregory,' right?"

"No," he confessed, "for 'MacGregor.' My maternal Grandmother was a MacGregor, and she named her daughter, 'Lois MacGregor Svenson.' 'Thibault,' of course, came years later."

"MacGregor. I'll call you MacGregor when I want your attention."

"Okay." He was parked by now, but this discussion was more important. "Now, early on, I told you the story of my parents' death and that my brother had taken over the company. My parents left an estate that was divided essentially into quarters. It had to pay estate tax. The major shares of that wealth were a house, quite a nice house without any impediments, shares in the family firm, insurance, stocks, and other bonds.

"The insurance was paid to the estate, and by the time that the taxes were paid, it and the other stocks and bonds were all gone, and we owed a little more. The house is still standing, and I officially own a quarter share in it. The stocks in the family company pay me exactly $30,000 a year."

"That much?" she asked. He knew that Anne was working full time and not drawing anywhere near that.

"That much. It went to the last of the estate tax at first, and to pay tuition and school expense. After I got a job, I had one hell of a lot more income than my fellow workers."

"I can see that."

"Not that they don't draw more than that now, but my contemporaries owe student loans. I, of course, pay more tax than they do. Then, too, I pay a quarter of the real-estate tax and some of the repairs on the house. The after-tax income from those stocks is something between $20,000 and $25,000 a year. Well, I live a bit above what my salary provides. I go on expeditions without applying for piddling grants. That takes some. I put maybe ten K a year into a couple of mutual funds."

"That sounds like a fortune," she said.

"Well, it's far less than a fortune, and because my brother Norm votes the stock, it would be a bitch to sell. Still, I have a fair chunk of change salted away, and that, of course, produces income as well. And everything I've salted away can be sold or withdrawn.

"Anyway," he finished up, "what I'm saying is that planning the wedding means planning the wedding beginning the marriage of a couple with some $10,000 of unused discretionary income every year. If you wanted to spend twenty or thirty K on the wedding, I wouldn't blink."

"I would."

Anne thought that blinking wasn't the worst of it. She'd faint before the first thousand was spent. She was still thinking that when they went into the jewelers. He could make the ring smaller, and he did. Greg paid him.

"Anyway," Greg said as they came out, "we are getting married in about a month. Then the issue will be how we will live. Up to then, the issue is how you will live. I'll be doing about the same as I have been.... Unless, of course, you would want to come to Boulder to live until then."

She thought about that. It sounded too good to be true. "I don't think so, Greg."

"I didn't think you would." He opened the car door for her and went around to his side.

"This has been wonderful," she said, and it had been wonderful. Partly because she kept going back to the real world so that she would know that she wasn't dreaming. "But I'd feel like a kept woman."

"Or, you could live here with any change you felt desirable. You could quit the restaurant and move into the hotel. You could quit the restaurant and live in your room. You could live in the hotel and keep working in the restaurant, although that would look weird to me."

It would look weird to anybody. "I don't think so, Greg. I think I'll go on as I have been." She wouldn't really go on as she had been planning to. She had been looking for another job, if not desperately and not since she knew Greg was coming over Thanksgiving weekend. The restaurant only took forty hours a week, and they were definite that they wouldn't increase her hours. Now, she would keep those hours and spend the rest of her time planning the wedding.

"Okay," he said. "I'm letting you decide your life. But, the wedding is something else. The wedding is the first step of the couple, Mr. and Mrs. Greg Thibault. For the wedding, you have those resources. Do you have a checking account?"

"Yeah." She didn't like the jump from their resources to her resources. She trusted Greg. She had trusted him with her virginity, and she trusted him when he said he would marry her -- two things Mom would have haunted her for if Mom had known Anne had trusted any man about that. When he said he had all that money coming in, though, it was as if he had said he flew to the moon by flapping his arms. Disbelieving him wasn't distrusting him; it was trusting reality more.

"Okay, when we get back to the hotel, I'll write you a check. Put that in your account. You know budgeting. Give me a week's warning before you need more." When they got back to the hotel, though, they got involved in other things. He didn't mention it, and neither did she.

Greg was determined to continue his policy of kissing all of Anne. When they were both naked, he took one more long, wet kiss. Then he had her lie down on her face. He was to her left, and he had hardly kissed her right shoulder blade at all. He started at the top near her spine and kissed a line going towards the shoulder.

When she was lying like this, her rump stuck up enticingly. He stroked it while continuing the kisses. When he ran the backs of his fingernails across it, it stuck up further and grew harder. Of course, it wasn't the only thing sticking out and growing harder, but he would ignore his erection for now. Ladies first, or, rather, lady's first.

Anne thought the idea of being kissed all over was sexy. The experience was less so. The problem was she couldn't do anything while she was lying on her stomach. Her arms, even, were under her to hold her off the bed enough to ease the pressure on her breasts. His fingernails on her seat, however, were arousing. When he tickled the insides of her thighs, it was even more arousing. She needed more and spread her legs to get it.

Then he stroked the folds between her legs. He moved his kisses to her spine, and parted the folds he had been stroking. She was feeling quite hot, now, and tried to turn over. He had his mouth on her back, however, and his hairy chest on her shoulder. She couldn't turn, and she soon concentrated on the sensations.

Heat was pouring off his finger and filling her lower regions. Then he seemed to bite her neck, and stroke even more firmly. Fire shot through her, and her muscles jumped. She pressed against the mattress, but she didn't seem to move. Then she didn't have the energy to move.

Greg kissed her neck one more time. Then he kissed each vertebra of her spine down to the small of her back. He kissed the mounds of her sweet rump one at a time. He lay down on his side, watching her face with his hand on her far shoulder. Finally, she smiled.

"We have only one more day here," he said. "I'll clearly have to leave some parts until after the wedding."

"You are silly," she said. She smiled, though. "But you didn't..."

"Didn't yet," he said. "Should I?"

Anne thought that question was as silly as the kisses. They were lovers, and they should be making love. "Oh, yes."

"Stay there." As he got between her legs while she was lying on her face, she thought for one second that he would enter her seat. She didn't want that, but she didn't want to refuse him, either. Then his fingers parted her folds. She felt him there, and felt his stomach on her seat. "I love you," he said. Then he pressed in.

She was stretched, as he always had stretched her. He didn't go in as far as he had previously, though. As he began to move in and out, it wasn't as far in as she had become used to him moving. Each motion stretched her entrance.

It felt different, but it felt arousing. Her seat was warm from his body heat pressed against her, and her stomach was hot from his friction within. The fire shot through her and raised her middle from the bed. The fire pushed her so hard that she lifted Greg.

Greg was excited at the new sensations of being in Anne so shallowly. Her lovely, hard rump supported his belly as he rolled on it to push in and out. Then she squeezed him inside her and raised his middle.

He shouted, "Anne!" He thrust hard and poured himself out. He could still feel her squeeze him as he emptied himself.

Anne was pushed down hard into the mattress by her seat. She could feel her entrance contracting around him, relaxing, and contracting again. When she collapsed, she could barely breathe, and she was carrying all Greg's weight on her back.

Greg finally moved off. "You," he said, "are so sexy." He kissed the middle of her back again, and one cheek of her rump before she rolled over. He kissed the hair on her mound. Then he moved up on the bed and kissed her mouth before lying back.

"One thing we haven't decided is what we'll do after the wedding," he said. He removed and discarded the Trojan.

"Why do I suspect that you already have an activity planned?"

"Well, that's what we'll do, if not, unfortunately, all the time. The question is where. We could take a conventional honeymoon. I don't mean, necessarily conventional in the sense of going to Niagara Falls. I mean people often schedule a trip then. We could, for that matter stay in this hotel again. We could go back to my apartment in Boulder. My family usually gathers in Minneapolis for the Christmas holidays. As three of us are in school in various ways, teaching, undergraduate, and med school, we tend to spend a long time there."

"Is my asking for a wedding right then going to interfere?" she asked.

"Not in the least. Actually, that way, attending the wedding and going to Christmas will mean three legs of a journey instead of four for two of them. But you will have to decide whether you want to spend a dozen of your first married days in my old room in a house that my stuffy brother runs."

"Well, I would get to know them," she said.

"You could, indeed, do that. And, after all, we would have a great excuse to leave."

"You know, you had both family and money. You, at least, recognize the advantages that having money gave you. I had a mother, period. I learned too damn little about my father, and those were all lies. I only heard that I had a grandmother when she died. Mom tried to fill my life, but she was in the diner every minute."

"You had a hard time," he said.

"No." She didn't want his sympathy. At least, right now, his sympathy wasn't the main thing she wanted. "I didn't have a particularly hard time." Though, of course, almost all of her friends growing up had either more family or more to spend than she had -- many had both. "You had a particularly good time. You had both parents; there were four of you kids; I'll bet you have new clothes. I'll bet your younger brother even had new clothes."

"Not all the time. We wore our clothes until we outgrew them or wore them out."

"And then you went to the store, not the thrift shop," she said. "But that isn't what we're talking about now. I want to be part of a large family."

"Do you want to go to Minneapolis for your honeymoon?"

"To your house? Yes."

Greg didn't think that would be much of a honeymoon for her. He said, "Then that's where we'll go," though. Well, she had a car. They could drive that back to Boulder before flying east. That would give them a night or two in motels, maybe a night in the apartment, before they had to share their lives with his cacophonous clan.

And, aside from the arguments and the somber mourning on the anniversary of his parents' death, Christmas at the Thibault house was fun. His gifts this year would be from Greg and Anne. He kissed her.

Anne kissed him back. They lay there kissing and stroking each other, but not being serious about it, until she needed to get ready for work. When she came out of the bathroom, showered and bare, he kissed her again. Then he handed her a slip of paper.

"Forgot about this," he said. "Why don't you put it in your purse? I suppose you can't deposit it until Monday." It was a folded check. Greg had his glasses on and he was watching her. Maybe he had forgotten the check; maybe he preferred to have her undressed so he could watch her walk to her purse to put it away. Greg tried to be sneaky that way, but he was utterly transparent.

When she was fully dressed, he drove her to her room. They had a nice kiss before she went in. Once upstairs, she looked at the check. It was for $1,000. She tucked it back in her purse -- as safe as any place in the room -- and got dressed for work. They had another kiss before she went into the restaurant.

Greg found a parking space when he'd let Anne off at the restaurant. He called Karen.

"Hello Greg," she answered.

"Karen, can you talk? Is this a good time?"

"It's fine. So why are you making Anne work?"

"I'm not," he answered. "She's at work this very minute. Can't you see that I'd rather be in a hotel room with her than in a car talking to you? No offense, but..."

"Well, she told me that she'd be waiting tables next year -- next academic year."

"I suggested the studying, and she was pleased. Then she asked about jobs as a waitress in Boulder. I know shit about that, though I've seen enough that I know there is a market. Look, I'm walking on eggshells. I love a free spirit. I do not want to lock her up. Well, I might want to, but I don't have the slightest suspicion that I could. I want her to fly free and come home to me when she has done her thing."

"And her thing is waiting tables?" Karen sounded suspicious.

"I brought a whole bunch of material with me about getting a degree -- I think she's going for two degrees, really -- from the University of Colorado. She was pleased. Then she brought up waiting tables. I suggested, as gently as possible, that she shouldn't do it this coming semester. I figured that this period of studying without other work would lead to a discussion of how much easier study was when you're not working part time -- easier, and more successful in terms of grades, and letting you deal with the broader aspects of student life. I damn-well don't want to tell her that being an archeologist is significant, but that being a waitress isn't. She's been a waitress every day since she was what? A high-school freshman?"

"Greg, nobody waits tables to be significant. You want to eat; you want to sleep off the streets; you want to wear clothes, new clothes sometimes. That's why you wait tables. People pay you to do it, and pay you the least that they can get away with, too."

"Okay," Greg said. "That's settled. I'll suggest that she doesn't have to be a waitress anymore. Damn it! My wife can eat, sleep dry, and wear new clothes. Now, have you two figured out the wedding, yet?"

"You don't object to it being in Tempe?"

"The only advantage that I see in Boulder is that I'm going to be there for the rest of the year. I would love to sling Anne across my saddle, ride off to Boulder, and never again let her out of my sight."

"You ride?" Karen asked.

"No. And that's not the only objection to that scenario. A woman deserves the wedding of her dreams once in her life. I don't want Anne thinking she could get it with a second husband. Anyway, I have family, but not in Colorado. They'll fly in, or not fly in, to Tempe as fast as to Boulder. Do I get the picture that it's really flying into Phoenix?"

"Yeah. The two cities are close."

"Anyway, now that we're engaged," he said, "I can give Anne money directly. I already have, but I've got a good balance in my checking account right now. I can send her more by electronic transfer. I'll tell her that tomorrow in front of you, if I can. Mind a visit from us?"

"No, I'm free."

"I suspect we'll be sleeping in. We'll call you tomorrow, and not when Anne gets off work in the wee hours. I'm depending on you. I've told her my financial situation, but I don't think it has sunk in. Anne's definition of rich is that you get your clothes in stores instead of thrift shops. All that matters is that you persuade her that she can have the wedding she wants."

"And you're rich?" she asked.

"Not really. But I'm a bit beyond the point of merely shopping in stores. I fly first class, for instance." Of course, he didn't fly first class when he was flying with colleagues. He wanted them to think of him as an academic, not as an inheritor.

"Greg," Karen asked, "you do know you were her first?"

"Well, that's no surprise." He hadn't actually known it, but she hadn't, certainly, acted as if she'd had any experience. "I'm more interested in being her last, though."

"Well, that's all in your hands. Right now, you're everything to her. Be good to her, and she'll be good to you."

"I certainly intend to," he said. They closed with that.

He got a hamburger before going back to the hotel. He stripped and lay down for a while in the dark. Partly, he dozed. Mostly, he thought about Anne. He showered and shaved before he went to pick her up. They had a meal at the restaurant after closing time. They returned to her room for her to change. Then they were in the hotel room for their last night together for a long time. Okay, it would be weeks on the calendar, but it looked like a very long time for him.

He kissed her as he removed her clothes. Then she lay down and he kissed her breasts while he worked on his own clothes. Sometimes, he had to move away from her to get some things off, but then he was naked. When he got into bed with her, he kissed her deeply while he cupped her mound.

Anne felt like Greg was holding all of her in his hand. Then he stroked her with his fingers. Heat spread from his mouth and from his hand. She had been tired, but she was wide awake now.

His tongue explored her mouth, and his fingers explored the folds between her legs. The heat spread, and she began to pant into his mouth. Suddenly, he pressed one finger deep into her. He kissed her neck and the heat spread from there to her face and breasts. He brought his finger out of her and up over her most sensitive part.

When he sucked her nipple at the same time, her whole body burst into flame. She shuddered as she felt the flame lick her. Then he was sucking the other nipple, and she could feel several fingers push into her. She felt herself clamp over those fingers. When she relaxed that clamping, the fingers pushed deeper. She felt a difference when she clamped again.

When she sank into the bed, unable to move, he still had his fingers deep into her. Greg kissed the parts of Anne that didn't seem involved in breathing -- shoulder, forehead, arm, other shoulder. By now, he was kneeling on the bed over her. When she seemed to recover, he pushed her head to the side with his own head and kissed her ear. It was so complex, and he traced the whorls with his tongue. As her breath became more even, he kissed her breasts and moved his fingers against the folds they were parting.

Anne felt the heat spread again, and -- as it did -- Greg returned to kissing her face. He kissed all over it until she reached up and brought his lips to hers. The kiss was breathtaking, and the heat spread again. While he pressed his face between her breasts, his fingers never stopped moving. She felt the tension of each of her muscles. She pressed her arms and legs into the bed and raised her middle into his hand to get more of those fingers. She could feel the tension, and it seemed to go on forever. Then the fire shot through her again. She shuddered and shook.

When she collapsed, he raised his face and looked into hers. What he didn't do was remove his hand. Soon, the fingers were moving again; the heat was rising again; she felt her body tense again.

Greg watched Anne's lovely face turn plain and worried. Then, as he continued to stroke her, her expression turned to that of pain. She grimaced, and her body went into a spasm with her feet pointing down and her arms flopping about.

When she stopped this time, she looked absolutely limp. Her face looked blissful, and he could see a rash spread across her face and down to her breasts. Her body, though, was as lax as though she were dead. He turned off the lamp, lay back, and molded her against his left side with her head on his shoulder. Any fears that she wasn't alive were allayed by her deep breathing against his side. He brought his arm down her back and held one buttock in his hand.

He took much longer to get to sleep than she did, but the feel of her rump in his hand and her breasts against his side made this time quite pleasant for him.

When Greg woke, he headed immediately for the bathroom. He relieved himself, shaved and brushed his teeth. He sauntered back into the room ready to kiss Anne awake. She, however, was ahead of him. As he came out, she grabbed something and headed into the bathroom. After noting that the condom was available on the night stand, he lay back in the bed. He covered himself with the sheet, but his thoughts were so concentrated on Anne that this did little to disguise his state. Well, Anne had never objected to his having an erection, even when she hadn't had any use for them.

Anne was as conscious as Greg that this was their last morning. She had brought the nightie in the bathroom with her. She relieved herself, showered, and brushed her teeth. Then she dried herself carefully, put on the nightie, let down her hair, and brushed it out. She figured that her delay was doing something to Greg. Well, he had aroused her and aroused her the previous night. He could stand a little arousal, himself. She consciously swished her hips as she came out of the bathroom into the room.

Greg had only seen the nightie once before. How a covering, even such a slight covering, could make Anne look even sexier than she did naked, he couldn't understand. But she did look sexy. He grabbed his glasses, and she looked even sexier. Her breasts were confined and her nipples were covered. The cloth was so sheer, however, that her breasts looked larger straining against their confinement and her nipples were more prominent pressing out against that sheer cloth. Her mound was sometimes covered and sometimes revealed. Even when it was covered, the naked legs below will lead the eye up to the where her center must be. And then, on her next step, the mound flicked into view. As it flicked out of view, the brief glimpse was seared into his memory.

He tossed the sheet aside and reached for the condom.

Anne could see that she had succeeded in arousing Greg. Men were so obvious, and Greg was lying on his back. He wasn't trying to hide it either; he removed the sheet to let her see it towering up from his middle. She realized, too, that she had also aroused herself. The slinky walk that flipped the bottom of the nightie to conceal and reveal her genitals also rubbed her folds against each other.

So, as she got closer and closer to Greg, the two bodies approaching each other were -- still out of touching range -- also approaching arousal. She knelt on the bed, leaned over, and gave him a wet kiss. As his tongue dueled hers, he tugged at the bow holding the nightie together. Her breasts spilled out, and the nipples, incited by the scratchy material, pointed towards him as though seeking his lips.

When she broke the kiss to breathe, he half lifted her by her lower ribs. He guided her over his body and then down until his lips touched her right nipple. That was throbbing before he moved her so that he could suckle on her left. She was now kneeling with her knees on each side of his chest. He ran the back of his nails up the insides of her thighs. The sensation was so erotic that she shivered.

Then one hand was cupping her right breast supporting it with his palm while his thumb brushed over her nipple. The other was holding her mound. She could feel the warmth spread from his hand through her lower belly. That thumb was delving within her folds, so exposed in this position.

The heat spread through her, and she stiffened. As she raised her shoulders, his lips fell from her breast. They looked at each other's face as he continued stroking and stroking.

When the flame flashed through her, she jumped. Then she crumpled onto him. Her breasts hit his face, and he turned his head to kiss her left one. He held her with one arm around her back and one hand grasping her seat. When she recovered her breath, she eased back. He was smiling at her, or maybe leering. She smiled back. Right behind her, he was still poking up, and he was covered with the contraceptive, too.

"Do you want me to?" she asked.

"Yeah. I want you a lot."

"I would never have guessed." Men were so blatant! She moved back until she was over him. When she settled down, he came between her legs. She moved a little up in the bed and eased herself down on him again. When he touched, she raised up a bit and grasped him with her right hand and herself with her left. When she eased down this time, she spread herself and fit him right in.

Greg watched Anne position them. Then he felt her surround him with her softness. Down, down, she went around him. When he was deep in her warm welcome, she straightened up. He looked from their place of joining up to her face. She was smiling and looking somehow triumphant. Indeed, looking down at him like this, she looked like a queen. He was certainly her conquered territory.

"You are magnificent," he said. Then she rose up again.

Anne felt full in a new way when she sat on Greg's hips. She felt wonderful, and a look at him reassured her that he felt good, too. The problem was that she had to provide the movement now. She tried, changed position once and tried again. Then she found a motion which gave her a special thrill. She held herself just so, and she moved herself just so, and the heat spread through her with each motion.

Then Greg touched her with his finger just above where he was going into her. It was her most sensitive spot, and the heat redoubled. She had him in her for less than a minute when the flames shot through her. She gasped and trembled, but she had lost control of her motion.

Greg felt her most feminine muscles gripping him, relaxing, and gripping him again. He couldn't hold still. He thrust upward, lifting her off the bed. When he dropped down, he came out a bit through one more grip of her insides. That made him thrust into her even harder and erupt.

Anne felt Greg pulse within her pulses. Then she felt nothing. When she came back, she was lying in his arms, and he was totally out of her. She slowly got herself arranged beside him.

"That's the last time I make love to Miss Anne Bernard," Greg said. "Or, at least, it's the last time I have sex with her. Our next time, we'll be married."

"Yeah." 'Married' was such a nice word. Much nicer than 'last time,' but she wasn't going to criticize his words. She got up. Greg removed the contraceptive and tossed it in the waste basket.

"Look," he said. "This is the timeline as I see it. My plane leaves a little after three. First, we check out. Then we have breakfast. Then we get your stuff back to your apartment. Then we go talk to Karen. Then we come back and I leave you at your apartment. Finally, I go to the airport and return the car. Work for you?"

Well, his leaving her in her room before he went to the airport didn't work for her, but she would argue that later. They each washed, then they followed his agenda. At breakfast, she called Karen and arranged to meet.

Greg parked by her place and helped carry her bags up to her room.

"While we're here," he said. "Do you have a spare check for your account?" She got one and handed it to him. He wrote 'VOID' across it in big letters. When they went downstairs, she thought she saw the manager's door twitch. She walked straight ahead as though she hadn't.

She told Greg how to get to Tempe and then to Karen's dorm. When they got there, some of the girls she knew were around. They admired her ring, paying much more attention to it than to Greg, who was standing right there. Then Karen came down, and they went out. It was too early for lunch, especially for Greg and her. So they drove and then parked with her and Karen in the back seat.

"Okay," Greg said. "There is going to be a wedding. It's too long in the future for my choice, but it will look damn soon when you start to plan it. The hard work is yours, and I hope Karen's, too. All I have to do is invite my family and write checks. Now that I have your blank check, I know how to move money from my account to yours through ETF, Electronic Transfer of Funds. That can be instantaneous for the guys who really know how, but expect me to take a day or two, a business day or two."

"You've already given me more money than the wedding will cost," she said.

"Well, you have more than a justice of the peace and a marriage license would cost, but I want you to have anything you want. You won't, obviously, have your mother there."

Anne said, "Well, that was her fault." Mom had been really critical of Greg.

"She can hardly be blamed for dying when she did," Greg said. "If she had been healthy, our romance would have gone faster, but I don't think it would have resulted in a marriage in the summer -- an engagement then, maybe." She thought about that. When did she know she loved Greg? When did she know he loved her? Really, she had always known he wanted her, but she hadn't been sure about his love until he had come to the funeral.

"You're kinder to her than she was to you."

"Maybe. But she could tell I wanted to take you away from her, and that was when she needed you the most. After all, you're not only beautiful; you're strong and brave. Partial credit has to go to the way she raised you."

"I suppose," she said. Sometimes, she missed Mom awfully. Sometimes, she remembered all that Mom had made her go through.

"Anyway, what can you two tell me about the wedding now?" Greg asked. And Karen was full of suggestions. Some of them sounded great; some of them she vetoed. Karen suggested having Prof. Barret give her away.

"Would he?" Anne asked.

"Well, I don't know. But you enjoyed his course so much. Don't you think you should ask him?"

"And," Greg said, "tell him that you are going to complete your course work, if not at Arizona State. If he liked you as a student, he'll at least want to know that. Trust me."

"He really is a teacher, Karen," she said. "Show her your ID." Greg passed over his faculty card, and Karen looked at it.

"Such a solemn young man," Karen said.

"That's how I was trying to look. I'd been a student, and I bought a new suit and a new haircut for the job interview. That was the suit, but I'd had to wait so long that I had to get a new haircut."

"Thanks for the ideas, Karen," Anne said. "It sounds like you've been thinking about this longer than I have."

"Well," Karen said, "first of all, I've been planning a wedding for a decade. Sure, we're different people, but some of that applies. Second, with the level of your planning, somebody who didn't know you as well as I do would say that you might have been distracted."

"Karen!" She felt herself blushing.

"Of course," Karen said, "I would never think that. You know," she was addressing Greg now, "you're getting the only girl in our class who still blushes."

"And she does it so delightfully, too," he said. It is absolutely impossible to stop blushing while sitting in a car with two people who are talking about your blushes.

After a little more discussion, Greg took them to lunch. He asked for restaurant suggestions, and she took him to a campus cafeteria. It was half-empty on Sunday, but several of the girls there recognized her and came over. They admired the ring and, at least, looked at Greg.

Then it was time for Greg to catch his plane. He didn't argue about her seeing him off. They had the longest kiss outside security, with Greg's tongue deep in her mouth and his hands clutching her seat. Then he turned and got on the plane. She couldn't bear to watch it take off, and she left for her room immediately.

When she got off work at the restaurant, she had a text message on her cell. Greg had landed and was safe back at his apartment.

Karen still had classes, and she had the restaurant, but they managed to get things together. Two other girls, Rebecca and Olivia, agreed to be bridesmaids. The Baptist Church and its minister were available for the ceremony, even on Sunday afternoon. Greg and his family could have got there Saturday, but not for the rehearsal. Prof. Barret seemed pleased by the request. Greg was right that Prof. Barret was happy to hear that she was going back to school.

"Don't you have anyone else to give you away, though?" he asked.

"Well, I never knew my father, and my mother died this fall."

"I heard that. My sympathy." He seemed to wonder about the wedding this close to the funeral.

"Well, Mom would have been happy about the marriage." Which was true enough. She certainly was convinced that Greg would never marry her. "I figured that, once it was decided that I would marry Greg, it would be hypocritical to put it off to show respect for someone who really wouldn't have wanted me to put it off."

She got the marriage license. Everything was set up. Greg insisted that there be a reception and a rehearsal dinner. He would pay for the rehearsal dinner -- not that he wasn't paying for the rest, but he would pay with his own credit card instead of transferring money to her.

Her last night at the restaurant, the other staff threw a small party for her after closing.

He had his family coming in, and they were all going to be staying in the same hotel as Greg had used before. He had even arranged for Mr. and Mrs. Greg Thibault to share the same room they had shared before.

All of his family were coming in on the same plane. She and Karen went to greet them in her car while Greg drove his rental car. They got off the plane together, and Greg had the greeting party lined up. He introduced her to Norman, and then she introduced Norman to Karen. Meanwhile, his sister, Diane was giving him a hug. When this was over, he introduced Diane to her, and Diane gave her a hug, too. She introduced Diane to Karen, who escaped without a hug. At that point, Ross was standing in front of her.

"Do I get one of those?" he asked.

"You get to kiss the bride at the reception, A.T.," Greg said. "Any attempts at other times, and I kick your butt."

"Hello, Ross," she said. She stuck out her hand, far out. He grinned at her response, but he didn't try to kiss her. She introduced him to Karen, having to interrupt Norman to do so. Ross picked up two pieces of carry-on luggage, and she led Greg's family to the luggage carousel. Greg stayed behind to meet his best man, Raj, who was coming on another plane. At the carousel, Norman got his own, and Diane told Ross which piece was hers. He fetched it. Anne was starting to wish she had had a younger brother.

She commented on that while they waited for Greg. Diane and Ross said nice things about each other. Norm and Karen were having their own discussion a few feet away. When Greg and Raj joined them, there were more introductions. At least Raj had only his carry-on.

"The ladies came in Anne's car," Greg said. "We thought that we'd need two for the luggage.

"Why don't I go back with them?" Norm asked.

"Legs," Greg said.

"Really," Norm said, "do you think I'd fit sidewards in your back seat, Anne."

"That way," Karen said, "there'd be plenty of room." Now, while Karen had spent a lot of time in her car, it was Anne's car. Then, too, Karen wasn't what you'd call an expert on leg room. Still, she and Greg accepted the division.

When she drove her car up to the pair waiting with Norm's luggage, though, Karen got in the back seat. Norm addressed them both on the drive, but Karen had most of the responses. She thought, briefly, of warning Karen about Norm. Most of what she knew, though, was Greg's report that he was a stuffed shirt. That was hardly a secret vice.

At the hotel, the family and Raj checked in. She used the time to bring another two pieces of luggage from her car to the room. Raj took Karen to the end of the hall to learn what his role was. Meanwhile, everybody else gathered in Norm and Ross's room. (Greg had thoughtfully asked them to put his family and Raj on a different floor than the one he and she would be on.)

"I was sorry to hear about your mother," Diane said. She didn't say, although she clearly thought, that it was too soon after the funeral for a wedding.

"Thank you," she said. "You're wondering about the timing. Well, Mom's illness, much more than her death, puts a real crimp in our romance. My friend, Karen, always said that it was all right if you were truly in love. Mom said, no, you shouldn't sleep with a man before you were married. Well, once I was sleeping with Greg, Mom would have wanted me to be married to him. At least that's the way I saw it. It seemed weird to delay the marriage because of Mom when she would have wanted it."

"You're probably right," Diane said. Norm looked curious, and Ross looked embarrassed. Then they all went to Tempe for the rehearsal.

Before that began, Greg and Raj did a little bonding with Prof. Barret over all of them being college faculty.

Greg had checked with Anne that Prof. Barret had taught the course on how plagues had changed history. He mentioned that.

"It was Karen who said that you were Anne's favorite teacher. I keep discovering that Anne tells her more than she tells me. Anne did, however, mention that course a long time ago. I had asked her what her favorite course had been."

"Well, we try to understand not only what happened, but why it happened," Barret said. "Even in terms of what happened, plagues are more important than changes of dynasty. You see a coin once in a month and a new coin less often than that, and who has his face on the new coins isn't of consuming interest. When half your village dies, you tend to notice that."

"Especially," said Raj, " when you're part of that half."

"There is that. Now, Anne tells me that she is going on in her studies."

"Yeah," Greg said. "Changing schools and missing a semester are both problems, but they are, in a sense, complementary problems. She took Arizona History, and she'll need Colorado History instead. Well, she'll take Colorado History this coming semester, along with two other courses. Whether she'll take anything in the summer, we'll leave till then. But when she passes the courses she'll take the spring semester, she will be on track to finish with one more year's courses."

"You think she'd be interested in going on?" Barret asked.

"As of now, she has a specific motivation for teaching high-school history. Grad school? That isn't on her present agenda. If the teaching experience disappoints, then that is something I'm perfectly ready to suggest."

"I'm surprised," Raj said, "you haven't suggested a change in major."

"To Archeology? Well, I'd love to have her for a student, but I clearly can't have her for both a student and a wife. So, I had to choose."

Then the minister came out and they all had to take their places. Things went well. He and Anne had agreed that, with everything going on and everyone running around, she would stay in her apartment that night. Anyway, he wanted the wedding night to be special.

Anne had heard of women deciding on their wedding day that the marriage was a terrible mistake. For all her nerves that morning, the marriage to Greg was the one thing that she didn't doubt. Really, did they need that large church for the few people that she knew were coming? And the minister had seemed a fiery preacher the two times she had talked to him. Would he decide that the gathered party was fertile grounds for evangelism? Would everything work? Would she look good in her wedding gown? Would she get hung up in the dressing and be too late for the event? Would Greg get cold feet and leave her at the altar? Would she break out in giggles when the minister asked "Do you, MacGregor..."?

Well, nothing did go wrong. The only problem was that her nerves kept her from eating much of anything before the service. So, she drank her champagne at the reception on an empty stomach. Before that, Ross and a score of other men had their kisses from the bride. She had more friends among the girls at school than among the boys, and the reception was almost two-to-one female. The dancing began with a her and Greg in a waltz, despite the fact that she didn't know how to do one, and neither -- they discovered -- did Greg. The dances after that, though, were the ones that he knew. She followed his lead and found it very pleasant. She was still in her wedding dress, and the songs went well with that costume.

"Y'know," Greg said, "I hadn't realized until the music started playing that we never danced together before this."

"There is so much we haven't done together."

"Well, we'll have the opportunity. I don't want, however, to do only new things. Let's not give up driving out in the country next summer and looking at the stars."

"That was nice," she said. "Do you mean that wasn't only an excuse to get me alone with you in the dark?"

"Not only." They laughed. Maybe it was the champagne, but it sounded funny at the time. Even at the reception, she didn't eat much. There was so much else going on. She didn't really drink that much, either. She was giddy, though, when they escaped through a hail of rice to the car. Ross drove them back to the hotel in the car Greg had rented. He let them off and went back to get the rest of the family and Raj.

Then they were in the room alone. It wasn't the first time that they had been together in a bedroom. It wasn't even the first time that they had been together in this bedroom. It was, however, terribly official. Up to then, they had been breaking the rules in order to have sex. Now, the rules said that they were supposed to have sex.

He helped her off with the wedding dress, then handed it to her to hang up. He stripped off some of his fancy clothes before turning again to her. He kissed her before removing the slip. A little later, he was still dressed below the waist while she was wearing only her panties. She lay on the bed while he stripped completely. He got the contraceptive out of the box in the drawer of the night stand and lay it within reach.

Then he got into bed with her and kissed her again. He kissed down to her breasts, and he spent a lot of time there. When he finally licked her nipples, she felt heat spread through her. He kissed down her torso. When he reached her belly button, she raised herself so that he could pull her panties down. Then he was kissing up the insides of her thighs from her knees.

Even before he got to her center, she was hot from knowing where his mouth was headed. Slowly, his tongue opened her up. Slowly, it licked from the bottom of her folds to the top, and then -- above the top -- to her most sensitive point. As the heat spread, her hands went and tangled in his hair. She felt them pulling him tighter against her center.

The heat filled her. Then, suddenly, the flame shot out in all directions. She thrashed, pulled his hair, kicked her feet. The sensations went on and on. When they stopped, so did her motion.

Greg had spent the last two weeks remembering the time on the blanket far out of town. "First" -- "Second." That had been special; that had branded her as his. And, now that she was branded in another and a more public way, he wanted to repeat that.

He lay with his cheek against her thigh. He breathed in the odor of her arousal and -- he would swear there was a subtle difference -- the odor of her completion. Her only motion was her heavy breathing, and he waited for more. While he waited, turned his head to kiss her thigh.

When she shifted, he kissed up that thigh toward her center. When he got there, she responded again. He licked the lip to his right; he licked the lip to his left; he licked straight up the center and all the way to her most sensitive point. He heard her breath catch at that.

Anne expected him to enter her when she recovered. She even thought that she needed him inside her. Instead, she felt his lips and tongue on her folds again. Both her hands were still tangled in his hair, and she almost pulled him up her body. Then the feelings were too good, and the heat spread too far. She lay back and basked in the heat.

His arms were suddenly along her sides, and then his hands were cradling her breasts. She could feel every stroke of his tongue; every stroke gave a thrill of pleasure; every stroke increased the heat. She was surrounded by Greg, his arms around her hips, his face holding down her center. Still, within that embrace, she writhed. The heat was overwhelming.

Suddenly, fire filled her. She pulled him hard against her by his hair. She slammed her legs down flat, pressing his arms beneath them. She shook, trying to escape the fire. Still more fire poured up and down from her loins.

Then, the fire was gone, and so was she.

Greg kept sucking on her clitoris until she stopped moving. He lay the side of his head on her mound. She lay still, shivered, lay still, shivered again. Then all the movement he could detect was her slowing breathing.

"I love you, Anne," he said. "I love you, Mrs. Thibault. I love you, beloved wife." That word sounded so nice. "Wife ... wife ... wife. You are, you know."

"Married," she agreed.

Anne knew damn-well that she was married. Even in her present dazed state, that was one thing that was clear. Most of the rest of objective reality was hidden in a blurring fog of sensation and lassitude. Then, the sensations began again. He stroked her breasts and rubbed her nipples. He kissed her mound through the curls before delving back into her center.

The thrills returned; the heat, which had never really dissipated, increased again. She tugged once at his hair without result. Then she spread her fingers and lifted her hands. She pressed her hands, her whole arms, against the mattress as the sensations flooded through her. She was so sensitive from the previous responses that every stroke of his tongue felt like it was rasping. Still the sensations were pleasure, not pain.

The heat was spreading, and his mouth was unrelenting. She wriggled under his mouth, not knowing whether she was pushing herself into his kiss or trying to escape it. He stroked both nipples at once, and licked all over the top of her slot.

She felt the heat expand until she couldn't escape it. Then the flame burst forth from her center. She felt pain in her nipples and flame burst down from that pain, too. She felt waves of flame flow through her, and she felt herself flow on those waves. The pleasure was so intense it turned to pain, but it would not stop.

And then it did. She lay replete, convinced she would never move again.

Greg moved his head from where he had been sucking on her clit. Then he moved his hands from her breasts where he'd pinched her nipples so briefly. He untangled his right arm from her leg and reached for the condom on the night table. He got the packet to his left hand -- that arm was still under her leg -- and tore it open. He rolled a little more to his left and put the condom on.

He moved over Anne using his left arm to lever her knee up until it was near her breast. That presented her center as a marvelous target, and he brought himself to her entrance. He pressed into her and raised her other leg with his right arm.

He felt himself deep in her. He extracted his left arm and then began to turn to that side. He grasped her rump to pull her against him as he turned.

Anne felt totally filled. As she felt the lower section of her body being turned, she turned herself so that she was lying on her right side. His hand was clutching her seat.

Then he moved back and forth, into her and out again. The heat increased once again. He was deeper in her than ever before, and the heat was spreading from a deeper point, too. When the fire came, it was a more gentle fire, but it filled her completely.

"Oh," she said. Greg pulled her harder and thrust against her faster. She felt him throb deep within her. When they both relaxed, he wasn't heavy on her at all, though her leg was trapped. Soon, they relaxed so much that they rolled a little apart and he came out.

When she woke in the night, the lamp was still on and her leg was still trapped. She extricated the leg, went to the bathroom, and turned the lamp off before getting back in bed. Greg snuggled up against her when she did.

"Married," she thought. She went to sleep with this word in her head.

The End

Here is a sample from another story you may enjoy:

Saving Heather

HOT ROMANCE EROTICA

LILITH JONES

She went into his arms. Her kiss had been intended to be a light acceptance of his niceness. He kept it up, though, and she certainly had no reason to end it. He sucked her lower lip, and then he licked her lips. She opened them to him, but he kept licking them. She finally sought his tongue with hers. When they met, sparks flew. He pulled her to him, and she felt his firmness against her stomach.

"Oh, my love," he said when they broke. His hands went to the buttons on her blouse. She was his, and she let him strip her. He did it slowly, kissing every newly revealed inch of skin. She felt aroused, more aroused than she had been in years. She also felt cherished, cherished as not even the Rick of years ago had cherished her.

When he was kneeling and he had her jeans down around her ankles, he eased back to let her step out of them. Then he kissed her legs upward to her panties. He kissed her mound through those panties, and she felt ready for him. He eased her down on the bed.

If he'd been patience personified in removing her clothes, he was nearly a blur in removing his. Then he faced her, fully nude and magnificently male. He looked as ready for her as she felt ready for him. She pushed the panties down, and Rick took them off her feet. She spread her legs slightly as he got into bed.

He started with a kiss, though. It was a gentle, but extremely sensual, kiss. She arched her hips off the bed as their tongues met. He cupped her, holding all her femininity. As he moved his mouth from hers to her breasts, her nipple strained upward towards his mouth. He licked it, touching only the tip with the tip of his tongue. She quivered all over, and he moved to the other breast. When he sucked that nipple, sparks shot from the tips of her toes.

He thrust one finger deep inside her. Then he drew it out, very slowly, and over her clit. It was only one finger, but it went so slowly that it felt much more -- maybe a yard long. He changed breasts again and sucked deeply. The sucking and the stroking were sending heat through her. She felt as though she was being baked, and there was a fire in her womb.

He raised his head from her breast and stared into her eyes. "Heather," he said. "Heather, my love."

Then lightning crackled within her. She moaned and writhed. It went on as he kept stroking. She collapsed, and he removed his finger. He kissed her forehead and her shoulder. As her breath eased, he kissed her nose tip, and then her breasts, and then her stomach.

He again stroked her mound. He rubbed the lips there against one another, very softly. The response, however, was fire. His hand was wonderful, and his look was loving if it was searching. He had brought her delight, and she could believe he would bring her more delight. She wanted more than that, though.

"You," she said. "Please!" He rolled away suddenly. She stifled a protest when she saw that he was reaching in his drawer. She almost told him that he didn't need the rubber. She could tell, though, that this was one more act of caring. He was taking responsibility, taking care of her. Whatever the physical shortcomings, she would celebrate it as an action of the man who would never put her at risk.

Now, he was kneeling between her legs. She spread her lips with her hand and rolled her hips to receive him fully. She felt open to him.

"Heather," he said.

"Yes, oh yes."

However open she had been, she felt him stretch her more as he went in slowly. And it was slow, agonizingly slow. When he had filled her, he kissed her briefly. She hugged him with her arms and with her legs. He was in her, but she wanted to hold all of him.

He withdrew as slowly, and he felt a need for him to return. He thrust in a little faster, and she felt herself burn. As he sped up, it was never fast enough. She thrust up to engulf him as he came down. Then the lightning crashed through her again.

He withdrew half way, rammed into her, and pulsed deep within her. For a second, he was one rigid arch within her hug. Then he collapsed onto his elbows. She, too, relaxed. Her feet rested on his calves, and her hands rested on his back, but she was no longer really hugging him.

That was closeness. They were one. She was disappointed when he moved away, although the freedom to breathe was a relief. He moved off the bed and turned off the overhead light. As he came back, she heard the rubber drop into the wastebasket.

"We really need another pillow," he said as he got into bed. He lay down beside her and pulled her into a hug. He carefully spread the sheet over both of them.

"We don't really need a wider bed, though," she said. He chuckled. "Y'know . . . Maybe you don't know. I'm on the pill."

"Well, it didn't seem a good time to ask."

"It wasn't. You took care of me."

"I always will," he said. "Somebody should. You work too hard taking care of Anne. Somebody has to take care of you."

"Well, maybe, we'll take care of each other."

"That's a good idea. I love you. Seriously, if we're going to be a family, we'll have to divide up the family tasks. Probably, you should do the dividing. But give me some of the tasks of caring for Anne. Just because I don't know how, doesn't mean I can't learn."

"You do great. I might have to give her the baths and wash her clothes, but you give her kisses and protect her."

"Washing her clothes and yours can't be all that different from washing mine, and I wash mine already. Anyway, first you get the divorce, preferably with full custody. Next we get married. Then, if I can, I adopt her. After that, we'll try to get her to call me Daddy."

"I love you." Heather thought Rick's project to get Anne to call him Daddy reflected more of the story that she'd heard at the funeral than Anne's situation. Right now, Anne had two men in her life. One beat her, and she called him Daddy. The other hugged her, and she called him Rick. Anne would know which name meant love. Well, courts took forever, and four-year-olds were resilient. By the time Rick had gone through his agenda, Anne would call him anything he wanted.

"And I love you, too," Rick said. She believed him. His hand stroked up to her breast, and she patted it and held it there. "Is this what married people do?" he asked. "I mean lie in bed and talk later?"

"Well, I'm not sure that I want my last marriage to be a model." And that was an understatement. Too many of her conversations with Bill had been at the top of their lungs. "Is this what you want our marriage to be?"

"Yeah. Especially this part."

If you enjoyed this sample then look for **Saving Heather.**

Here is another sample you may also like:

SHYLA STARR

LOVE
Anew

LONELY BILLIONAIRE ROMANCE SERIES, BOOK 1

Tricia reached for another blanket. "Are you cold?" she asked.

Rebecca's breath was raspy as she responded. As her lungs shut down due to ALS, or Amyotrophic Lateral Sclerosis, her ability to speak had started to decline. Muscle by muscle, ALS targeted the body and made it impossible for the individual to live a normal life. It had started a few years ago with Rebecca's legs. Now, her lung muscles were starting to freeze as well. Tricia winced as she thought about the future. If Rebecca chose to use machines to stay alive, her entire body would eventually stop working. At some point, her mind would remain functioning and she would be locked into her body.

Rebecca managed to squeeze out a feeble yes. Reaching over to the cupboard, Tricia removed a blanket and carefully tucked her in. Tricia had spent years training to be a nurse and really liked her job. Since she was an excellent nurse, she had caught the eye of the billionaire, John, at one of the couple's many trips to hospitals around the country. He had noticed the love and care she took with each patient. After a moment's hesitation, Tricia had allowed him to convince her to take care of his wife.

Pictures of Rebecca dotted the room. Since she was unable to leave, John had striven to make her room look like favorite memories of her life and activities. A young, healthy Rebecca smiled in each photo. In the few years she had been physically active, she had acquired awards for horseback riding, cooking and other projects. Now, though, this time of physical fitness had passed. Instead of dashing through the fields on her favorite horse, Rebecca spent her time in this room. She had taken her difficulties in stride and was truly brave in the face of all of these medical issues.

Finishing with the blanket, Rebecca started to say something. Leaning closer to hear her, Tricia finally pulled up a chair. "What do you need, Rebecca?" she queried.

Sighing, Rebecca whispered, "I need to talk to John. I have to tell him how I want to die."

Squeezing her hand, Tricia nodded. "Once I leave your room, I will go get him. Just in case he is not around, did you want me to give him a message?"

Rebecca tried to nod, but her head did not respond all the way. "Yes, I do. You need to tell him that I do not want any machines. He could keep me alive forever with a breathing tube, but I do not want to live a life where I am permanently locked into my body. And," she paused and struggled to take another breath. "I do not want him to stop enjoying life or waiting around for my eventual death. If God wants to take my soul now, we should not interfere."

Tricia nodded sadly. Most patients with ALS were more afraid of being stuck within their minds than actual death. She understood, but she could not imagine what life would be like without Rebecca's gentle soul. "I will tell him," she said.

Leaving the room, Tricia traversed the hallways of the mansion. John had built his fortune by buying and selling real estate properties. His initial money had arrived through an early investment in the dot com boom before the bubble burst. After seeing the dangers of the stock market, he had started to just buy and rent out properties. Even with the recent recession, he still made a profit. Instead of selling his properties or developing, he had continued to rent them out. In a decade or two, he had talked of selling and retiring. His plans had arrived before his wife had been diagnosed with ALS. Unwilling to speak of his life after her future death, Tricia had not asked about any change in his future plans.

Knocking on the door, she heard a sound in the room and assumed that he was telling her to come in. She entered the office and John motioned for her to sit down. His tousled brown hair fell softly across his face and his icy blue eyes were focused intently on paperwork in front of him. Between running an empire and worrying about his wife, he seldom took time any more for his personal appearance. His face was growing a rugged stubble and looked like it had not seen a razor for a while. Dashing and muscular, his good looks had an almost otherworldly level of gorgeousness. John was known among business associates for his confidence and aggressive tactics. He played fair, but he managed his company with the best of his abilities.

If you like this sample, look for **Love Anew - Lonely Billionaire Romance Series, Book 1 by Shyla Starr.**

Also by this Author:

<u>**Saving Heather**</u>

From the Author

If you enjoyed any of my books then please share the love and promote my books in Amazon.

If you write me a review and send me an email I will send you a free book, or many.
(Just know that these emails are filtered by my publisher.)

Good news is always welcome.

One Last Thing, For Kindle Readers...

When you turn the page, Kindle will give you the opportunity to rate this book and share your thoughts on Facebook and Twitter. If you enjoyed my writings, would you please take a few seconds to let your friends know about it? Because... when they enjoy they will be grateful to you and so will I.

Thank You!

Lilith Jones
lilith_jones@awesomeauthors.org